R.L. STINE

HORROR HIGH

FATAL KISS

■SCHOLASTIC

Scholastic Children's Books
An imprint of Scholastic Ltd
Euston House, 24 Eversholt Street
London, NW1 1DB, UK
Registered office: Westfield Road, Southam, Warwickshire, CV47 0RA
SCHOLASTIC and associated logos are trademarks and
or registered trademarks of Scholastic Inc.

First published in the US as *The Girlfriend* by Scholastic Inc, 1991
First published in the UK by Scholastic Ltd, 1992
This edition published in the UK by Scholastic Ltd, 2009

Text copyright © R.L. Stine, 1991

ISBN 978 1407 11148 3

British Library Cataloguing-in-Publication Data
A CIP catalogue record for this book is available
from the British Library

The right of R.L. Stine to be identified as the author of this work
has been asserted by him.

Printed in the UK by CPI Bookmarque, Croydon, CR0 4TD
Papers used by Scholastic Children's Books are made from wood grown in
sustainable forests.

3 5 7 9 10 8 6 4 2

www.scholastic.co.uk/zone

One

"I'd like to propose a toast to Jack and Lauren," Mr DeMarco announced. He raised his fluted champagne glass above his head and held it there until the large, crowded room grew quiet.

Jack tried to hide behind Lauren, but she turned and pulled him beside her, her expression playfully scolding. "This is embarrassing," Jack whispered.

"Get used to it," Lauren told him, holding him in place with both hands so he couldn't escape. "My dad *loves* embarrassing people. It's his hobby."

"I know, I know," Jack replied, shaking his head, his eyes on the front of the large rec room where Lauren's dad was still holding his champagne glass in the air, waiting for all the guests to raise their glasses.

Jack and Lauren had been a couple since sixth grade, so Jack knew exactly what to expect from her parents. Both of them were warm, and outgoing, and generous. Too generous, Jack sometimes thought.

They smother you with kindness. That's how he sometimes described them.

Jack felt smothered by this lavish party, with the enormous, seemingly endless buffet table, the overstocked bar, the five-piece band out on the terrace, the young waiters parading around in their black dinner-jackets, carrying silver trays of salmon and caviar hors d'oeuvres.

After all, it was a little too early to celebrate.

Jack and Lauren had received preliminary acceptance at Princeton, but nothing official yet. And Jack might not be able to go anyway. He was still waiting to hear about his scholarship.

Jack and Lauren had urged the DeMarcos to wait a while before having the party. For one thing, it was only November. They still had the rest of their senior year at Glenview High to finish.

But, Mr DeMarco, in typical fashion, had insisted on throwing this huge, expensive party. "Don't worry about it," he had said, his youthful face beaming happily, one big arm around each of them, crushing them both in an affectionate hug. "We'll throw another party after the school year. Or maybe *two* parties – one for each of you!"

Jack and Lauren finally gave up trying to discourage him.

"What's the point?" Lauren asked, as they were sitting in the front seat of her father's BMW, parked up by Rainer Point, overlooking the town. "Dad will always be Dad."

"But it's so rubbish!" Jack exclaimed unhappily. "I mean, throwing a party for us for no reason."

"I wish you wouldn't say 'rubbish' all the time," Lauren said, squeezing his hand affectionately. "I mean, we're going to Princeton, you know – not just any old uni."

They both laughed.

"You're a snob," Jack said.

"And you love it," she replied and kissed him for a long time.

Jack did love it, he had to admit. He liked everything about Lauren. He liked how her wavy, blonde hair caught the sunlight, how soft it felt in his hands. He liked staring into her wide, hazel eyes. He liked the way people said she looked like a model, like a young Kate Moss.

He liked walking down the hall at school with her, holding hands. "You know we're a cliché," he'd tell her. "I mean, the football quarterback and the Homecoming Queen? Get real!"

"I don't feel like a cliché," she'd reply in her serious way. "I just feel like me."

He had to admit he didn't at all mind that they were a cliché. Being with Lauren always made him feel good. And he was proud of being the starting quarterback of the Tigers.

He'd been voted player of the year last year. That was pretty good.

Jack liked the fact that everyone thought of him and Lauren as a couple. And he liked the fact that other kids were jealous of them. And of him. He didn't think about it a lot, but when he did, he admitted to himself that having this long, steady relationship with one girl was maybe the most admirable thing about him.

Other kids, even his best friends, even Walker, his very best friend, seemed sort of aimless to him. Immature.

Jack liked being responsible. Maybe it was because his father had been so irresponsible. Running off without a word, leaving Mrs Singleton to bring up Jack and his younger brother Charlie.

How could he *do* that to us? Jack often asked himself.

He never came up with a satisfactory answer.

Lauren's parents seemed to have such a close, stable relationship. Maybe that was why Jack liked them so much.

He realized he liked being with the DeMarcos as much as with his own family. When he didn't feel smothered by their wealth, by their enthusiasm, by their generosity.

Now he found himself looking around the large, brightly-lit rec room, crowded with kids from school, relatives of both families, and a lot of people he'd never seen before, and *definitely* feeling smothered.

"We should never have agreed to this," he whispered, leaning against Lauren.

"We had no choice, remember?" she whispered back, as her father rambled on with one of his endless, meandering toasts.

"But it's so embarrassing," Jack moaned, staring across the room at his friend Walker, who was leaning against one of the sliding glass doors, staring back at Jack with his eyes crossed and his tongue hanging out of his mouth.

"Don't think of it as a going to Princeton party. Think of it as a going-away party for me," Lauren said, playfully stepping down hard on his foot until he winced in pain, her eyes straight ahead as if concentrating on her father's toast.

Jack was tempted to pour his Coke down the front of her dress, but managed to hold himself back.

He had almost forgot that Lauren and her parents were going away. Off to Paris for a week. Mr DeMarco had some sort of architectural business to take care of, so why not turn it into a spur-of-the-moment family holiday?

He glanced at his mother, in her flowing fuchsia-pink dress, which was just a little too tight on her plump body, her platinum hair piled high on her head, standing in front of Mr DeMarco, glass in hand, listening so intently.

For a brief moment, Jack felt real envy. He wanted to be in

the DeMarco family. He wanted to go on unplanned trips to Paris, too.

Oh, well, some day soon, I *will* be a member of the family, he thought, glancing affectionately at Lauren.

". . . I'm so proud of these kids . . ." Mr DeMarco was saying at the front of the room.

And then Mrs DeMarco looked away from her husband and gasped.

Mr DeMarco stopped abruptly in mid-sentence. All eyes turned to where his wife was staring – to the buffet table, where Lauren's little white cat had leaped up and was enthusiastically sampling a good helping of the salmon mousse.

"Oh, Fluffernutter!" Lauren cried, letting go of Jack's hand and rushing towards the buffet table.

One of the waiters got there first and lifted the still-chewing cat off the table, setting it gently down on the tiled floor.

"I think that was a sign that I've been talking for too long," Mr DeMarco said, grinning. He held up his glass one more time. "To Jack and Lauren," he announced, looking for Lauren. He couldn't see her because she was down on the floor scolding her cat.

There was a clinking of glasses, and conversations resumed around the room. Jack breathed a loud sigh of relief, took a long gulp of Coke from his glass, and headed over to thank Lauren's dad for the toast, even though he hadn't really heard much of it.

"Hey, man," Walker caught his arm. "Watch out for those caviar thingies. I tried one, but it tasted really fishy."

"I'll be careful," Jack said dryly.

Walker was tall and lanky, the tallest one in the room even though he was only seventeen, and still growing. He should've played basketball, Jack thought. He never could figure out why his friend wanted to be a footballer.

"What kind of a party is this without any pizza?" Walker complained, only half serious.

"It wasn't *my* idea, man," Jack said, sighing. "You want to go out for a pizza? I'll go with you."

"Yeah. Sure," Walker said sarcastically, glancing down at Lauren who was still on the floor playing with Fluffernutter, unaware that she was getting white cat hair all over her dress. "You ready for Friday night?"

Jack nodded. What with all the excitement over being accepted at Princeton and the party, he hadn't had much time to think about the game. "Lincoln isn't that good," he said.

"They're ace!" Walker exclaimed, pushing his heavy, black-framed glasses up on his narrow nose. "They beat Westerville thirty-five–nil, and we could only tie with Westerville."

"They got lucky, man," Jack said, grinning. "They're rubbish. Totally rubbish. We can take 'em."

He saw Mr DeMarco coming towards him, so he slapped Walker's hand in a low five and started to push his way through the crowd to meet him.

Mr DeMarco, chewing a fried chicken drumstick, beamed at Jack, raking back his thick, brown hair with one hand. He's so proud of his hair, Jack thought. He's always telling everyone how he's forty-five and still has every hair on his head.

"Hey, thanks for the toast," Jack said, trying to sound enthusiastic.

Mr DeMarco brushed chicken crumbs from his wide red tie. "I think I went on a bit too long, but I just couldn't help it." He flung an arm around Jack's shoulder, nearly knocking Jack over. "I'm just so proud of you two!"

"Thanks," Jack said uncomfortably.

"You know, I have a little bet on the game on Friday night," he said confidentially, his arm still around Jack's shoulders, guiding him towards the hallway that led to the rest of the house.

"You're betting on Lincoln?" Jack joked.

Mr DeMarco stopped for a moment, then laughed. "No way," he said. "You're going to take the Tigers to the state championship. I know it."

"Well . . . I don't know," Jack said, feeling his face grow hot. "We've got some tough games. And with Jergens hurt . . ."

"You just have to throw more," Mr DeMarco said. It was one of his steady themes. Jack was too generous, he was always saying. Jack should forget about sharing the glory. He should throw the ball more. The team should ride on Jack's arm.

"I don't think Coach Hawkins would agree," Jack always replied.

"Who *cares* about Hawkins?" was Mr DeMarco's answer. "He's a chemistry teacher. What does *he* know about football?"

Jack never won this argument. He seldom won any argument against Lauren's father. Mr DeMarco was too powerful and too insistent. He never gave up until he got his way.

"Listen, Jack, I meant everything I said in that toast," he said, turning serious, his face close to Jack's. "Keep making me proud, son. I know you will. I know you and Lauren both will. Keep making me proud. You know, when you graduate from Princeton, there'll be a place waiting for you in my firm."

Jack's mouth dropped open in surprise. "Really?"

It was a generous offer. Mr DeMarco's architectural design firm was the biggest in the state and was rapidly getting a national reputation.

Jack planned to do architecture at Princeton. His dream

was to build amazing skyscrapers, to change skylines. Now it looked as if his dream would almost certainly come true.

"Thank you, Mr DeMarco. That's just awesome," he exclaimed. "I really don't know what to say."

Mr DeMarco was looking past Jack, back into the room. The glass doors had been opened. Outside, the band had started to play, and people were drifting out onto the large, flagstone terrace to dance. "I can't believe what a beautiful evening it is," he said to Jack. "Imagine? Twenty degrees in November? It's like spring out there. Luck just seems to rain down on you and Lauren."

"I guess so," Jack said, still thinking about Mr DeMarco's amazing offer. He said goodbye to him and headed excitedly over to Lauren, who was talking animatedly, circled by friends from school.

It took Jack a while to separate her from the group. Then he led her out onto the terrace, which was lit by pale pink paper lanterns strung around the sides.

"If the trees weren't bare, I'd think it was summer," Lauren said, taking a deep breath of the fresh, cool air. "What were you and my dad talking about?"

Jack couldn't hold in the news a second longer. He told Lauren about her father's job offer.

"That's so exciting!" Lauren cried. She kissed him enthusiastically.

Walking with his arm around her shoulder, he led her across the crowded terrace. The swimming pool was drained and covered with its winter canvas tarpaulin. He led her past it, past the small pool house and into the large, sloping garden, away from the lights and the music. They stepped over the wet grass, walking around the carefully trimmed evergreens and shrubs.

"I shouldn't have complained," he said softly. "It's turned out to be a great party. Totally awesome. "

"I think Fluffernutter stole the show," Lauren said, snuggling against him.

"Fluffernutter stole the salmon," he corrected her. "I should've brought *my* pet. That would liven up the party."

"Your snake?" She made a disgusted face. "Yuck."

He pretended to be hurt, as he always did when she insulted his snake. "I think Ernie is cute," he teased.

Lauren started to say something – but only managed a choked gasp as a dark figure, arms raised to attack, leaped out at them from behind a tall bush.

Two

Jack threw his arms up as the dark figure lunged at him, wrapping him in a tight bear hug.

"Charlie!" Jack yelped. "Are you *nuts*?!"

"You scared me to death!" Lauren cried, holding her hand up to her thudding heart.

Jack's seven-year-old brother let go of Jack, tossed his head back, and laughed. "Gotcha!"

"You got us, all right," Jack agreed, still feeling the effects of the shock. He reached forward and picked Charlie up off the ground.

"Hey – put me down!" Charlie protested, still laughing.

But Jack held his brother up over his head like a pair of weights and began to twirl him easily.

"Put me down! I'll puke on you!" Charlie screamed. "I had a big dinner, Jack! I'll puke on you!"

Jack quickly returned his brother to the ground.

"Hey – you're strong," Charlie admitted grudgingly.

"You're a featherweight," Jack said, straightening his tie and jacket.

It was true. Jack and Charlie didn't look at all like brothers. Charlie was short and slender. Jack was tall, broad-chested, with a thick football player's neck, muscular arms, and big hands. Charlie had curly black hair that he wanted kept very short because he didn't like it to be curly; small, dark eyes; and delicate features. Jack had straight, light brown hair that he kept short on top but down to his collar at the back, big blue eyes, and a large nose that looked as if it had been broken even though it hadn't. Charlie always looked serious. Jack seldom did.

"What were you doing behind that bush?" Lauren demanded, holding Charlie in place by pressing both hands against his shoulders.

"Hiding," he said.

"Hiding? Why?" Lauren asked, not letting him go, even though he was trying desperately to squirm away.

"To scare somebody. It's a party, right?"

Lauren laughed. Charlie scampered back out of her grasp.

"Charlie knows how to party," Jack exclaimed, putting his arm around Lauren's shoulder. She shivered. There was a chill in the air. "It's a party, so you scare someone."

"What *else* is there to do, stupid?" Charlie asked, sneering.

"Don't be rude," Jack said, frowning.

"Well, you're stupid," Charlie repeated. He said the word a few more times. It was his favourite word. He said it all day long.

"Why don't you go inside and play in the sour cream dip?" Lauren suggested.

"You're stupid, too," Charlie told her. He turned and ran back towards the terrace. "I'm going to tell Mum you two were kissing and stuff!" he yelled before disappearing into the crowd.

"He's so cute," Jack said sarcastically.

"He *is* sort of cute," Lauren said, nestling her head against his shoulder. He smelled her hair. It smelled of coconut.

"He's a shrimp," Jack muttered. "He'll never make the team."

Mentioning the team made him think of the game against Lincoln the following Friday night. "I can't believe you're missing Homecoming," he said, not meaning to whine.

"I know. But what can I do?" She shrugged. "I'll be thinking of you."

"In Paris," he said, rolling his eyes.

"You can beat Lincoln without me, Jack."

"No. You're my good-luck charm," he said, only half kidding.

"That's what I am?" she cried, pretending to be offended. "I'm a good-luck charm? That's why you keep me around?"

He nodded, teasing her. He liked it when her eyes lit up, and her face got all fiery. "That's all," he said. Then he quickly turned serious again. "You're missing the dance and everything."

"Oh, come on, Jack," she cried, giving him a hard, playful shove. "You don't care about the Homecoming dance, do you? You *really* wanted to stand up in front of all those gawking creeps – I mean, all of our classmates – and be crowned Homecoming King and Queen?"

He turned his glance towards the house. The band was taking a break, but people stayed on the terrace, standing in small groups, talking and laughing.

"I know it's all rubbish," he began.

"Yes. It's totally ridiculous," she interrupted.

"But it's kind of an honour," he continued seriously. "And it *is* our last Homecoming dance. I mean, we'll be graduating and everything. I mean . . ." His voice drifted off. He felt embarrassed. Everything he was saying sounded so nerdy.

She looked up at him, holding onto his arm, leaning against him, but didn't say anything.

"Well, you know how everyone expects us to be the perfect couple," he said. "I'll have to answer a million questions. 'Where's Lauren?' 'Why aren't you going to the dance?' 'Have you and Lauren had a fight?'" He shook his head. "It's going to be totally rubbish."

"Hey, I just had a funny idea," Lauren said, a sly grin forming on her face, her greeny-brown eyes catching the light from the half moon in the clear sky above them.

"Huh?"

"I think it would be really funny if you got a date for the dance."

He stared at her, his face filled with confusion. "What? What do you mean?"

She chuckled. "You know. Ask somebody else to the dance. It would be great. You'd show up with some other girl, and everyone would totally freak!"

He studied her face, trying to decide if she was serious or not. "You're kidding – right?"

"Of *course* I'm kidding," she replied. "But it *would* freak everyone out, wouldn't it?"

"You have a weird mind," he said. He wrapped his arms around her waist and kissed her.

The party ended a little after midnight. Jack's mother had taken Charlie home a few hours earlier. Now, suddenly feeling very tired, Jack said goodnight and thanked Mr and Mrs DeMarco.

Lauren, yawning loudly, walked him to the front door. "Don't look so sad," she said. "I'll only be gone a week. I'll send you a postcard from the Eiffel Tower. And I'll think of you all the time. I promise." She gave him a long, sweet kiss.

16

"See you in a week," he said despondently. He started out the door.

"Be good," she called after him. "Stay out of trouble."

Trouble? Jack thought, heading to his car. What a strange thing to say.

How could *I* ever get into trouble?

Three

Jack stormed into the locker room and heaved his helmet across the room. It hit a locker with a loud *clang* and bounced onto the floor.

"Come on, man," Walker urged, slapping Jack's shoulder pad. "We'll get 'em next half. It's not so bad."

"It's nine to nil," Jack growled, kicking his helmet hard as it rolled over to him on the cement floor.

"Hey, we'll catch 'em," Barker, a running back, yelled, sitting down on the bench across from Jack. "I almost broke one, you know. If I hadn't slipped . . ."

Jack looked towards the doorway as his team-mates entered, most of them downcast and silent.

I'm letting them down, he thought, picking up his helmet, inspecting the scratch he had made by heaving it into the locker.

I'm letting them down.

"We've been down before," Walker said, untying his cleats so he could tie them again. "It's no big deal."

"I know I'm going to break one," Barker said. "Just give me the ball over right tackle. Their whole right side is slow, man. I can get around 'em."

"I should have got rid of the ball," Jack said quietly to Walker. "I never should've let 'em get me in the end zone."

"It was my fault," Walker said. "I let that guy through. He just rolled over me like a tank. He must weigh a hundred and forty kilos. And he's only a sophomore."

Jack grabbed a paper cup of water and downed it. Then he took a towel and wiped the sweat off his face. From out in the stadium, he could hear the band going through its Homecoming routine. What was that song they were playing? "Zip-a-Dee-Doo-Dah"?

"I just lost my concentration," he said glumly, scratching his head. "I should've grounded the ball, just heaved it or something. Instead I stood there like a dork and ate it."

He reached into his locker and pulled out his black-and-silver Raiders cap.

I'm letting them all down, he thought. On Homecoming.

At least Lauren isn't here to watch me blow it.

Maybe that's the problem, he thought. Lauren isn't here to watch. At the party last weekend, he was only kidding about her being his good-luck charm. But it was obvious he performed better when he knew she was there, watching him, cheering him on.

Up at the front, across from the showers, Coach Hawkins slammed a locker with his fist, his usual way of getting their attention when they were losing at half-time. "You can beat these guys," he said, his high-pitched voice echoing off the low ceiling. "You just have to execute. It all comes down to who executes best."

"You wear that Raiders cap in the shower?" Walker asked, grabbing it off Jack's head and examining it.

Jack grabbed it back. "It's sort of a good-luck cap. Lauren gave it to me."

"Maybe that's your problem," Walker said, finishing with his cleats, leaning forward to grin right in Jack's face. "You're thinking about the dance."

"I'm not going to the dance," Jack said, his eyes on the coach, who was diagramming a complicated defensive formation on the small chalkboard.

"Huh? What?"

"You heard me," Jack said edgily. "Lauren is in Paris, remember?"

"I don't believe it!" Walker exclaimed, grabbing a plastic water bottle, tilting it over his head, and letting a stream of water run down his face. "The quarterback and the head cheerleader won't be at Homecoming?"

"You can go in my place," Jack said dryly. He tapped his hands nervously against the bench. He hated half-time. It was always his most nervous time of the game. "You got a date, Walker?"

"Yeah," Walker nodded, drying his face with a towel.

"With who?"

"I don't remember. I called so many girls. I don't remember which one said yes." He laughed.

Jack forced a laugh, but he was thinking about the game. And about Lauren.

My good-luck charm, he thought.

"Hey – did you hear me?" Coach Hawkins cried, glaring at Jack.

Jack looked up, startled. "Yeah, I heard you," he lied.

"Well, let's see you do it," Hawkins squeaked. "You guys can beat Lincoln in your sleep."

"We just can't beat 'em when we're awake!" Walker whispered.

"Let's get out there," Hawkins yelled, heading for the door.

"Go Tigers!" someone yelled.

"Go Tigers!" several voices repeated.

I've got to get up for this, Jack thought. I'm not going to be a loser on Homecoming. No way!

He jumped to his feet and stood up on the bench so the rest of the team could see him. "Let's kick their butts!" he shouted, gesturing with his helmet high over his head. "Let's kick their butts! Go Tigers!"

His cheers got them all shouting enthusiastically.

That's more like it, he thought.

Pulling on his helmet, he jogged out of the locker room, and led his team onto the field. His heart began to pound as he stepped under the bright, white lights, the cheers from the stands rising over the drums of the departing marching band.

He ran down the line of players, slapping everyone a high five, a tradition he had started. The quarterback has to be a leader, he told himself.

Now I'm going to show them I'm a leader.

Whoops of victory pierced the silence of the locker room as the Tigers swept in after the game, laughing, cheering, shoving each other, butting heads, a noisy, sweaty celebration that Coach Hawkins couldn't stop if he wanted to.

"We shut 'em out! We shut 'em out!" Walker was screaming, swatting his towel wildly at anyone who passed.

Well, we *did* shut them out in the second half, Jack thought, joining the celebration, chanting along with his team-mates. The final score was 14–9. But, secretly, Jack felt disappointed. The defence had been responsible for both Tiger touchdowns, scoring the last one on a fumble recovery in the final two minutes.

Of course, the stadium erupted into total bedlam. And Jack was thrilled that they were going to win. But happy as he was, Jack wished that he had had a little more to do with the Tigers' victory. He had played his worst game of the season.

I'm glad Lauren wasn't here to see this game, he thought, as he joined the raucous cheers, slapped hands, laughed and shouted with his team-mates, and pretended he was as happy as they were.

The only way Coach Hawkins was able to stop the locker-room victory party was by blowing his whistle until his round face grew as red as a balloon, and then reminding them that they all had to appear at the traditional Homecoming bonfire behind the stadium in less than ten minutes.

After a quick shower, Jack got into his jeans and T-shirt, pulled on his jacket and his Raiders cap, and started for the door, intending to hurry home and skip the bonfire.

"Hey – Singleton!"

It was Walker, pulling a green-and-white Glenview hoody over a T-shirt as he chased after Jack. "Wait. I'll walk to the bonfire with you."

"Is that what you're wearing to the dance?" Jack teased. "Couldn't you have at least found a *clean* hoody?"

"Hey, it's almost clean." Walker grinned. And then he added, "At least I'm *going* to the dance."

"You really are rubbish, man," Jack said, shaking his head. "You really know how to kick a guy when he's down."

"How can you be down?" Walker asked, pushing open the door. A rush of cold air greeted them, feeling even colder because they had just stepped out of a steamy shower. "We won the game, right? In spite of you." Walker laughed to show he was teasing.

"Hey, watch it," Jack said edgily.

"Friends have got to be honest with one another, right?" Walker asked.

"Wrong," Jack said.

"Oh. Then I take it back. You were awesome tonight," Walker said, grinning.

Jack punched him hard on the shoulder. Then the two of them began to jog around the car-park to the back of the stadium.

"Hey, we're just in time," Walker said.

Mr Velasquez, the principal, was holding a long, flaming torch, about to light the bonfire. A crowd of two or three hundred Glenview students, parents, and people from the neighbourhood huddled in hoodies, jackets, and winter coats, looking exaggeratedly bright and colourful under the high stadium lights.

Jack followed Walker up to the front. Planks of wood, branches, logs, sticks, rags, old cushions, newspapers, and assorted flammable items had been piled into a mountain nearly two storeys tall.

Across the way, Jack saw three Glenview policemen eyeing the proceedings warily, shifting nervously, their eyes on Mr Velasquez's torch. The Homecoming bonfire wasn't the police department's favourite event, Jack knew. One year, Jack's freshman year, the celebration had got out of hand, and a house had been set on fire.

"Turn off the lights!" Velasquez yelled. A few seconds later, the high stadium lights obediently faded out, surrounding everyone in darkness except for the orange-yellow light of the wavering torch.

A strong gust of wind blew past, bending the torch flame, pushing it downwards. The crowd grew silent, drew closer. Jack pulled down his Raiders cap, then shoved his hands into his pockets.

Get on and light the fire, he thought. It's getting cold out here!

Velasquez, with his usual dramatic flare, raised the torch high over his head, then lowered the flame to the pile of wood. The flames took hold slowly at first. Sticks crackled. A small yellow flame began to spread.

Before long, the entire mountain burst into flame, the orange-yellow light licking up towards the black, starless sky. It's really awesome, Jack thought, looking around the circle of cheering faces. Everyone looks so orange and warm.

He took a deep breath. It smelled so good. A branch crackled and broke, making a group of kids jump back. The flames leaped higher and higher. The fire had become a pulsating, yellow mountain, warm and alive.

"Who brought the marshmallows?" someone shouted.

It got a pretty big laugh.

Jack stepped a little closer, allowing the darting, bright flames to warm him. Velasquez tossed the torch into the fire, then raised his hands over his head, trying to get everyone's attention.

"We had a victory here tonight!" Velasquez shouted in his booming, deep voice. "Let's let the team know we appreciate them. Let's really hear it for the Fighting Tigers!"

This was the excuse the crowd was waiting for to go wild. A deafening cheer rose up, kids slapped hands, and hats and gloves were tossed into the fire. A shoving match started between a group of guys very near the fire, and the three policemen moved quickly to break it up.

The crowd started to chant, "Tigers! Tigers! Tigers!" And when the team paraded in a single line in front of the fire, the wild cheers and celebrating started all over again. Jack got the biggest cheer of all. He grinned and waved at everyone, holding his hands over his head in a double victory sign.

What a night! Jack thought happily. He wished Lauren were there. It would've been so much more fun with her.

And then suddenly the crowd was calming down again, and Velasquez, his face bright red in the glowing firelight, was starting to talk. "We have another bonfire tradition," he shouted.

Jack searched the crowd for Walker, but couldn't find him. Faces looked strange and distorted in the orange light. A picture of rows and rows of jack-o'-lanterns popped into his mind.

What was Velasquez going on about?

". . . when we crown the Homecoming King and Queen," the principal's voice boomed over the crackling and spitting of the fire.

What? Jack wondered. What is he saying?

"And so I'd like to call our Homecoming King and Queen up here right now!" Velasquez shouted enthusiastically. "Jack and Lauren – get up here where everyone can see you!"

"Oh, no," Jack groaned out loud. "Didn't anyone tell him?" He could feel his heart sink down to his feet.

"Jack and Lauren! Let's give it up for them!" Velasquez shouted.

Didn't anyone tell him Lauren isn't here? Jack thought. What am I going to do? This is so embarrassing.

As the crowd cheered, he realized he had no choice.

Slowly, hands shoved in his pockets, keeping his eyes on the ground, he made his way towards Velasquez.

Oh, please, let me die right here, he thought. Before the jokes start. Before everyone has a good time laughing at me.

"Lauren? Where are you?" Velasquez called when the cheers died down.

"She stood him up!" some guy screamed.

The crowd roared with laughter.

Jack felt his face grow hot.

"She had another date!" another joker added.

Another roar of laughter. At Jack's expense.

"Where's Lauren?" Velasquez asked Jack.

"She's in the car-park with Walker!" someone shouted.

The crowd thought this was hilarious.

Jack glared angrily into the fire. He had never been so embarrassed in his life, but he didn't want to let these clowns know they were getting to him.

"Lauren isn't here," he told Velasquez, leaning close so the principal could hear him over the crowd. "She's away with her family."

"Oh. Right," Velasquez said, slapping his forehead. "Someone told me that this afternoon." He turned away from Jack to address the crowd. "Lauren is away with her parents. What a shame! But at least we can crown the Homecoming King!"

Jack gritted his teeth and let himself be crowned with the stupid crown. He felt like a total dork.

Finally, after a few cheers by the cheerleaders, the bonfire ceremony was over. People started to wander off in groups, still laughing and cheering.

Jack tore off the crown and tossed it into the fire. Then, ignoring calls from a couple of friends, he put his head down and started to run at full speed towards the student car-park. His face still felt hot from the fire. The rush of air was cold and refreshing.

"Singleton – you going to the dance?" someone called.

"Hey – where's Lauren?" someone else yelled.

He ignored them and kept running. A car squealed out of the car-park, burning rubber as it roared off down Fairwood Street. "Good game, Jack!" a guy yelled from a car as Jack ran past. He acknowledged the compliment with a quick wave, but kept running.

His car, the old Ford his mum had bought second hand, came into view at the very end of the car-park. Jack slowed to a walk and reached into his jacket pocket for the car keys.

He was struggling to unlock the front door when he saw something down low against the fence.

It was a girl.

What was she doing down there? Was she OK?

Jack stepped back from his car and walked over to her. As

he came closer, he saw that she was on her knees, leaning over a bicycle, which was lying on its side.

She was wearing a thin, pale green jacket. Her back was turned to him. In the white light suspended over the car-park, he could see that she had long, red hair, which flowed down to her waist.

Hearing him approach, she turned her head and gave him a shy smile. "Hi." she said breathily.

Four

"Flat tyre?" Jack asked.

"Yeah." She made a face.

"That's really rubbish," he said, shaking his head.

She's very pretty, he thought. Her long, red hair falling loose behind her was really wild and sexy. And she had a high forehead, and big, brown eyes, and full, red lips.

He thought she looked very dramatic. Like an actress.

I've seen her around school, he thought. But he couldn't remember her name.

"It's a pretty cold night for a bike," he said.

"D'you want to buy me a car?" she cracked. Then she laughed to soften the remark. She had a light, breathy laugh, like her voice.

She got to her feet. He was surprised by how short she was. Her head didn't come up to his shoulders. She looked frail and light in the thin jacket, which flapped in the wind. "I

31

think it's a puncture," she said, and kicked at the tyre. "I'll have to push it home."

"How about a lift?" Jack said, pointing to his car. "We can toss the bike in my boot."

She looked so light and fragile, as if a strong wind might blow her away.

"Thanks," she said, her big, brown eyes examining him. "I'm Shannon Smith."

Right, he thought. Shannon Smith. He remembered her now. She had only been at Glenview for a year or so. He'd seen her sitting in the canteen by herself. She didn't seem to have many friends. He remembered her wild red hair.

"I'm Jack Singleton," he said.

"I know." She looked down at her bike. "Everyone knows *you*," she added, her voice a whisper.

He ran his hand through his short hair. He suddenly felt awkward, nervous. "So? Want a lift?"

Another car squealed out of the car-park, the kids inside yelling and singing, the radio blaring. He looked around. The car-park was empty now, except for him and Shannon.

"Thanks," she said. "I'm pretty cold." She bent over to pick up the bike. He helped her carry it over to his boot. Then he opened the boot and shoved it in.

She lowered her dark eyes, smiled at him, a teasing smile,

and slid into the passenger seat. He climbed in behind the wheel and started the engine.

"Aren't you going to the dance?" she asked, toying with a strand of her hair, tangling it and untangling it around her fingers.

"No," Jack said uncomfortably. He rubbed his cold hands together, waiting for the car to warm up.

"I don't have a date, either," she said softly, playing with her hair. She reached over and touched the back of his hand. "Thanks for rescuing me." Her hand was surprisingly warm. He could still feel the warmth of it after she pulled it away.

He backed up, then headed out of the narrow exit. Up at the school, he could see couples heading in to the dance. He looked for Walker, curious to see who his date was, but didn't see him.

I'm sure I'll hear all about it tomorrow, he thought.

He glanced over at Shannon as he pulled into the street. He liked the way she nibbled at her bottom lip. She glanced back at him, shyly.

"You were good tonight," she said softly.

"You mean at the game?" He shook his head. "I was rubbish. Totally rubbish."

"No, you weren't," she protested, letting go of her hair, dropping her hand to her lap. She scratched the knee of her jeans with slender fingers. "We won, didn't we?"

"No thanks to me," he said moodily, turning onto Park Street.

"Are you always so modest?" she asked, touching the back of his hand again.

Her touch sent a shock of electricity up his arm. "Where do you live?" he asked.

"At Sharpes Corner," she said, looking out of the window. "You know, in the Old Village."

"Yeah, sure," he said. He didn't go to the Old Village much. None of his friends lived there. The houses were old and small and close together. He remembered hearing on TV about a big effort to restore the Old Village to its former glory, or something.

"Do you like football?" he asked, glancing away from the road to look at her. She was playing with her hair again, winding it around one hand. He realized he was very attracted to her.

"Not much," she replied and then laughed at her answer. "But I like going to the games. My brothers all like football. I guess that's why I don't like it."

"How many brothers do you have?" he asked, slowing for the light at Harbour Crossing.

"Three," she said, making a face. "Three big louts."

"Let me guess," he said. "You don't like your brothers?"

"We don't have much in common," she said, sliding down in the seat, raising her knees to the dashboard. "They're all older than me. They're all big. Really big. The oldest one, Joe, was a pro wrestler. A pro. Do you believe it?"

"Wow," Jack said. "Remind me to stay on your good side!"

He had meant it as a joke, but he saw her face turn serious. "I will," she said softly.

They drove in silence for a while. She's so pretty, Jack thought. Why doesn't she have a date tonight?

"D'you want to stop and get a hamburger or something?" he asked. The words popped out. He hadn't really thought about it. As he said it, it felt as if someone else were talking.

I haven't been out with another girl in . . . *how many* years? he asked himself.

Never, he realized.

He'd been with Lauren since sixth grade.

Well, I'm not really *out* with Shannon, he told himself. This isn't a date or anything. I'm just helping her get home. So what's wrong with stopping for a hamburger on the way?

"I'd love to," she said breathily, her voice so soft he could barely hear her.

"Great," he said. "I'm always starving after a game." He turned the car around and started to drive to Henry's, the hamburger restaurant near school where everyone hung out. He had gone half a mile when he decided that wasn't a good idea.

There'll probably be a lot of kids I know there, he thought. And they'll see me with Shannon. And they'll start making jokes. Or they'll start making up stories about me. Or word will get back to Lauren that I had a date with another girl.

Why look for trouble?

"Know any good places in the Old Village?" he asked.

She nibbled at her bottom lip, her expression thoughtful. "Well, there's a Burger Basket on Ridge just before the railroad tracks."

"Sounds perfect," he said. "Let's go there."

"OK," she said softly.

Did she sound a little disappointed, or was he just imagining it?

A few minutes later, he found the Burger Basket and pulled into the car-park. There were only two other cars there, he noticed with relief.

This looks like a pretty rough neighbourhood, he thought, looking around at the low, dark buildings and empty car-parks across from the hamburger restaurant.

As they walked in through the glass doors, Shannon took his hand. Her hand felt so warm, so light, so fragile. She smiled up at him, a playful smile. Her hair smelled sweet, like cinnamon and oranges.

He guided her to a booth at the back, away from the windows.

Hey, I'm not doing anything wrong, Jack thought.

So why do I feel so strange?

Five

He liked the way she kept touching his hand as she talked. She was always gesturing with her small hands, tugging at her hair, reaching across the table to touch his arm or his hand, as if she had known him for years.

And he liked the way her red hair fell, tangled and wild. Lauren was always fussing with her hair. It had to be perfect, not a hair out of place. But Shannon didn't seem to care. She tossed her hair back over her shoulder as she talked, or twirled a strand around her fingers, or tugged at it, smiling, as she leaned forward to listen to him.

She smiled at him with those dark, pouty lips. Her smile was knowing, almost smug, not at all an innocent little girl's smile.

The restaurant was empty except for a pair of silent old men hunched over cups of coffee, and four tough-looking teenagers Jack had never seen before sitting in a booth next to the window.

He felt comfortable knowing that no one from school would see him here. And he felt excited sitting here with Shannon, a kind of excitement he had never felt in his life. The excitement of doing something wrong.

Or of *thinking* about doing something wrong.

Of course, he kept reassuring himself, there's nothing wrong with having a hamburger with someone and driving her home. It's not like Lauren and I are *married*, he thought, scolding himself for feeling guilty.

"You're a senior, right?" Shannon asked, wiping hamburger juice off her chin with a paper napkin.

"Yeah. You too?"

She nodded. "What are you doing after graduation?"

"Oh, I'm going to Princeton," he said casually. "Where are you going?"

She looked down. "Probably look for a job, I guess."

He could feel his face redden. She must really think I'm a rich jerk, he thought. Why did I assume she was going to college?

"I'm . . . uh . . . hoping to get a scholarship," he added quickly. "My mum can't really afford it unless I get a scholarship."

"Where's your dad?" she asked.

Jack was a little startled by the question. He responded with a broad shrug, as if to say, "Who knows?"

For some reason, this struck Shannon as funny. Her laugh was high and fragile, like the tinkling of a glass wind chime.

They talked for an hour after their hamburgers were finished. Jack was usually exhausted after a football game, but being with her was keeping him wide awake.

They didn't have much in common. She hated school, hated Glenview, seemed generally unhappy with her life but didn't have any plan for changing it. Unlike Jack and Lauren and their friends, she didn't seem to have any ambition, any goals, any dream.

When he asked her what she'd really like to do with her life, she had to think about it. Finally, tugging at her hair, she said, "I don't know. Be a rock star maybe. Maybe be like Madonna."

As he drove her home, she slid low in the seat, her knees on the dashboard. She turned on the radio and cranked up the volume until the entire car throbbed and vibrated, and sang along in her whispery voice, ignoring Jack entirely except to point the directions to her house.

The house was a little box, so small Jack nearly drove right past it. It was entirely dark. He drove up the dirt driveway, his headlights rolling over a rusted pick-up truck, tyreless, up on blocks in the middle of the narrow front garden. The house was white clapboard but looked as if it hadn't been painted for a long time.

Jack clicked off the blaring radio.

"Home sweet home," Shannon said, sighing.

How do her three big wrestler brothers fit into that tiny house? Jack wondered.

He jumped out, ran around the car through the twin white headlight beams, and pulled open the car door. She reached up her hands, and he pulled her to her feet on the soft dirt drive.

To his surprise, she didn't let go of his hands. Squeezing them tightly in her warm hands, she leaned forward, raised herself on tiptoe, and pressed her mouth against his.

Her lips were wet and burning hot.

Her soft hair brushed against his face.

She leaned forward, pressing against him. He started to back away, but realized she didn't want the kiss to end. Giving in to it, he put his arms around her.

She kissed harder, harder.

Hungrily.

Finally she let go. Backed away. Smiled up at him. That sexy, knowing smile.

Wow, he thought.

"Thanks for the lift," she said, breathing hard.

"Uh . . . no problem." He couldn't think of anything else to say. "Hey – almost forgot your bike."

He could still feel the heat of her mouth on his, could still feel the brush of her hair against his face. Feeling crazy and exhausted and excited and confused all at once, he walked quickly to the boot, opened it, and pulled out the bike.

"You can just leave it here. One of my brothers will fix it for me in the morning," she said, pulling the light jacket around her.

He set it down beside the drive.

"Shannon – are you busy tomorrow night?"

"What?"

He walked back towards her. "Do you want to go to a film or something?"

She smiled. The half moon in the dark, starless sky above them sparkled in her eyes.

I don't believe I just asked her out, he thought.

What am I *doing*?

"Yes. OK. Cool," she said.

"I'll come by about seven."

What am I *doing*?

She turned and ran quickly to the dark house without looking back. He climbed into the car, closed the door, and looked for her. But she had disappeared. Probably already inside.

The car bumped over the dirt driveway as he backed out into the street.

One date is no big deal, Jack thought.

Lauren is off in Paris having the time of her life. Why shouldn't I have a little fun, too?

Besides, Lauren will never know . . .

Six

Saturday was grey but not as blustery. It felt to Jack more like a day in late September than November. He had slept in, then had a long, leisurely breakfast. When Walker came over to help rake leaves as they had arranged, Jack was still in his pyjamas.

"You ill or something?" Walker asked, walking in through the back door without knocking, as usual.

He startled Jack from his thoughts about Shannon.

"You look pretty serious this morning," Walker said, grabbing a piece of cold bacon off Jack's plate and stuffing it into his mouth.

"Oh. I was just thinking about . . . the game," Jack said, thinking quickly.

"Great game," Walker said, wandering around the kitchen on his long, lanky legs, looking for more food to scavenge.

"Yeah," Jack agreed, trying to clear the fog from his head. "I'll get dressed. Be right back, man."

"Sure. I'll just make myself a sandwich or something," Walker called after him.

He eats as much as a herd of elephants, Jack thought in his room, pulling on jeans and a hoody. But he's the skinniest, lightest tackle on the team.

A few minutes later, they were raking the front garden, attacking the large, dead leaves with enthusiasm. "Hey, you guys," Mrs Singleton called, poking her head out of an upstairs window. "What are you doing?" She had a pink bath towel wrapped around her head.

"What are we doing?" Jack shouted up to her. "What does it *look* like we're doing? We're raking the leaves!"

"Well, why are you raking in one direction and Walker raking in the other?" she demanded. "You're making two separate piles!"

Jack and Walker looked at each other. "That's just the way we rake," Jack replied.

"The earth is round, Mrs Singleton," Walker added. "Jack and I are bound to meet sometime!"

"Very funny!" she called sarcastically, and slammed the window shut.

"No sense of humour," Walker muttered, leaning on the rake, then pretending to fall off it. He toppled sideways to the ground. Walker loved falling down. He thought it was hilarious. And he was very good at it.

"How was the dance?" Jack asked, thinking about Shannon as he started to rake again.

I can't believe I asked her out, he thought. Am I really going to go through with it?

Of course.

He realized he hadn't heard Walker's reply.

"Hey, everyone was asking about you and Lauren," Walker said. He was raking with the wrong side of the rake. Anything for a laugh.

"Stop messing about. We'll never get finished," Jack said, laughing.

"So what did *you* do after the game?" Walker asked.

"Oh, I just went home and . . . watched a dvd," Jack told him, avoiding his glance.

"Yeah? What'd you see?"

"Uh . . . I don't remember, man. It was just some stupid film Charlie rented."

I'm such a bad liar, Jack thought. I can never think fast enough when I want to tell a lie, and I bet my face is bright red.

Walker, raking in long, slow sweeps, didn't seem to notice. "So what are you doing tonight? Want to come over and play pool or something?"

"I can't," Jack said quickly. Too quickly.

Walker looked over at him. "How come? Hot date?"

"Yeah, sure," Jack said sarcastically, still avoiding Walker's eyes.

Walker laughed at the idea. "Lauren would murder you," he said.

"I . . . uh . . . have to do some schoolwork tonight," Jack lied.

One lie after another, he thought, feeling guilty.

"You? Work?" Walker exclaimed, and fell backwards into the leaf pile he had made. "I thought you got your perfect grades without cracking a book." He sat up. Flat, brown leaves clung to his hair. "Besides, man, they've already accepted you at Princeton. Why knock yourself out?"

"I can't just veg out for the rest of the year," Jack replied. "Then people would think I·was *you*!" He laughed at his own joke and tossed the rake to the ground. "This is boring," he said, helping Walker to his feet. "Let's go and check out Ernie."

"You still have that snake?" Walker asked, loping along behind Jack, around the side of the house to the back garden.

"Yeah. I built this cool cage for him," Jack said. "On the side of the garage. I put a heater in it and everything, and Ernie gets plenty of sun and fresh air. Mum wouldn't let me keep him in the house since he got so big. She's scared of him."

"Scared of snakes? How weird!" Walker exclaimed.

Jack gave him a playful shove. Walker pretended to go flying into the side of the garage.

They stopped in front of the large mesh-and-glass cage Jack had built. "Hey, you've practically got a whole tree in there," Walker said, peering in from the top.

"Well, Ernie's a tree snake," Jack explained. "I wanted him to feel at home."

The bright green snake was coiled up in the V formed by two branches, its head hidden from view.

"That's the most amazing colour," Walker said. "That green is almost neon. I'd like to have a shirt that colour."

"I thought *all* your shirts were that colour," Jack joked.

"Just the smart ones," Walker said. "So, how about it, Jacko – change your mind. Come over tonight. You can work next year."

"No, really, I can't," Jack insisted. "I've . . . just got shedloads of work to do."

Going out with Shannon has *got* to be wrong, he thought. And here I am, lying to my best buddy.

But so what?

So I'll be *bad* for just one night.

"Hey, Jack!" His mother yelled from the back door. "Jack – are you there?"

He stepped away from the cage. "Yeah, Mum!"

"The post just came," she shouted. "Come and look. You've got a postcard from Lauren!"

Jack pulled his Raiders cap low over his forehead as he and Shannon walked out of the cinema. "How'd you like it?" he asked, his hand on her back, guiding her towards the car.

He had taken her to the old Westside cinema in the next town, deliberately staying as far away as possible from the multiplex at the mall, or anywhere else he might be recognized.

"It was pretty cool," she said thoughtfully. "But I didn't get some of the humour, I don't think. It was very dry."

He had watched her during the film and hadn't been able to tell if she was enjoying it at all. For the most part, she sat through it, expressionless, nibbling on her lower lip. Near the end of the film, she had taken his hand between hers and held it tightly, staring straight ahead at the screen.

He couldn't help stealing glances at her. She was wearing a tight wool jumper and a very short leather skirt over sheer tights.

I can't believe I'm sitting here with her, he thought.

He was so nervous and excited, he could barely follow the film.

"I thought Will Ferrell was awesome," he said, trying to keep the conversation going. So far, it hadn't been as easy to talk to her as the night before.

47

"Will Ferrell. Is he the funny one?" she asked, lowering herself into the car.

Of *course* he's the funny one, Jack thought as he walked around the car and slid into the driver's seat. Who *else* would he be?

He was starting to think that asking Shannon out was a big mistake when, without warning, she leaned across the gearstick and kissed him.

She smelled so sweet, like oranges. Her hair brushed lightly against his face, tickling his cheeks, sending a chill down his neck.

She leaned back into her seat, smiling at him, licking her lips.

He took a deep breath. "Would you like to go up to Rainer Point?" he asked softly, suddenly feeling nervous. Everyone knew that Rainer Point was a big make-out spot. How would Shannon react to that idea?

Shannon laughed and shook her head no.

Jack felt embarrassed. Too fast, he thought. I moved too fast. That wasn't too cool of me. I'm such a dork! And now she thinks I'm a dork, too!

But then she touched the back of his hand and said, "Let's go to my house instead."

He looked over to see a very playful smile on her face. "What?"

"Let's go to my house," she whispered. "We'll be all alone. My brothers are away, and my parents are at an all-night party."

"Really?" he gulped, his voice cracking.

She nodded her head, her long hair covering her face. "Really," she said, pulling the tangles of red hair away.

He turned the car around and headed towards her house. The night was clear and cold. There were a lot of cars on the road, people out looking for fun on Saturday night. An accident at Penn Crossing had the traffic at a standstill.

They sat in awkward silence. She smiled at him. He tried to think of something to talk about. But they'd already gone over last night's football game again, and they'd already discussed the film, and school, and the weather.

He was grateful when Shannon reached over and turned on the radio. Again, she turned it up until the car felt about to explode, and sang along, so softly he could see her lips moving but couldn't hear her sing.

We don't have much in common, he realized. This will have to be our only date.

But she really is a babe!

When he reached her house on Sharpes Corner, he pulled up the dirt drive and turned off the headlights and the engine. The house was completely dark, as the night before.

As soon as they got inside, she slammed the front door.

Then, staring boldly, almost challengingly into his eyes, she pulled off his Raiders cap and tossed it across the dark room.

Then she started covering his face with kisses.

Wow! he thought. This is *awesome*!

"You're *my* baby now," she whispered, holding his head with both hands as she kissed him.

"You're *my* baby now."

Seven

Jack was woken up the next morning by the phone ringing. He stirred, shook his head as if trying to shake away his sleepiness, and pulled himself up to a sitting position.

Downstairs, he could hear the thunder of Charlie's trainers against the living room floor as he ran to answer the phone. "I'll get it!" he screamed.

Jack yawned and stretched. His head felt like a lead weight. When had he finally rolled back home? It must have been after one in the morning.

And what time was it now? He tried to focus on the digital clock beside his bed, but it was a blur.

"Jack – phone for you!" Charlie shouted from the foot of the stairs, loud enough to wake the dead. "It's a girl!"

"Huh?" Jack said aloud, scratching his head.

Could it be Lauren?

No. Her plane doesn't arrive until this evening.

He lumbered over to his desk, tossed a dirty T-shirt out of the way, and picked up the phone. "Hello?" His voice sounded low and husky.

The voice on the other end woke him up immediately.

"Good morning, baby," Shannon chirped.

"Huh? Shannon?" His throat felt dry. He realized his heart was pounding.

"I had such a good time last night," she said softly.

"What time is it?" Jack asked.

Why is she calling me? he wondered. What does she want?

"It's early, but I just wanted to talk to you," Shannon replied in a little girl's voice. "Did you dream about me?"

"Listen, Shannon . . ." he started. He could hear his mum padding down the corridor, coming towards his room.

"Are you coming over to see me today, baby?" Shannon asked in a tiny voice.

"No, listen. Shannon, I . . ."

Mrs Singleton poked her head into the room. Her platinum hair was piled high on her head, tied with a purple ribbon, but she was still in her dressing-gown. "Who is it, dear?" she asked, her expression disapproving.

"I'll have to call you later about that," Jack said quickly into the phone. "Talk to you later, OK?" He hung up the receiver. "Just a girl from school," he told his mother, trying

52

to sound nonchalant. "She had a question about history homework."

"So early?" Mrs Singleton asked, turning her disapproving gaze on the clock.

Jack could read it now. It was 8:08. Sunday morning.

"I guess she was getting an early start on it," Jack said. "I probably should, too."

He hated lying. Whenever he did it, he had the feeling lights lit up on his face, blinking on and off, "Lie! Lie! Lie!"

"When did you get in last night, Jack?" she asked, tightening the belt on the loose fitting dressing-gown.

"Not too late." Another lie.

"Well, I'm just going down to start breakfast. D'you want pancakes this morning?"

"No. Something light," Jack said, making a face.

He stood leaning on the desk, listening to her slippers thud down the stairs. He heard her ask Charlie what he was doing up so early. Charlie already had the TV on in the living room. Jack could hear the loud boings and crashes of some kind of cartoon show.

I've got to tell Shannon not to call, he decided.

I've got to make it really clear to her that it's over between us. I mean, we just had the one date. It was just a one-time thing.

When he had said goodnight to her, standing in the dark,

narrow hallway of her tiny house, he tried to let her know that he wouldn't be seeing her again. "I'll call you sometime." That's what he had told her. "I'll call you sometime."

The meaning of that is pretty clear, he told himself.

Shannon had smiled back at him in the dark, but she must have understood what he was telling her.

It was over, over, over.

After all, Lauren would be home tonight. He realized he couldn't wait to see her. An entire week was a long time without seeing Lauren.

Much too long.

He showered and pulled on a pair of grey joggers and a hoody. Maybe Walker and I can go to the park and play a little roundball, he thought. Shoot some hoops. Or maybe go on a long bike ride. He felt like getting some exercise.

He was down in the kitchen, finishing his cereal, sitting at the breakfast counter with Charlie and his mother, when the phone rang again.

Jack started towards the wall-phone beside the fridge, but Charlie got there first. "Who is it?" he asked into the receiver. Charlie never bothered to say hello. He always picked up the phone and asked, "Who is it?"

He held the phone out to Jack. "It's for you," he said. Then he grinned. "The same girl!"

Jack caught the surprised expression on his mother's face

as he hurried over and took the phone from his little brother. "Hello?"

"Hi, baby," Shannon said in her whispery voice. "Whatcha doin'? You didn't call me back."

"Uh . . . listen . . . uh . . ." Jack looked back at his mother and Charlie. They were both staring at him. "I'm going to take this call upstairs, OK?" he said. "It's homework stuff." He handed the receiver to Charlie. "Hang up when I get upstairs, OK?"

Grinning, Charlie took the receiver and held it up to his ear. "I can hear her breathing," he said.

"Just hold it for a second," Jack snapped. He hurried out of the kitchen, through the front hall, and up the stairs to his room, thinking hard about how to get Shannon to stop calling him.

"What does she think she's doing?" he muttered to himself aloud.

As he picked up the phone in his room, he was breathing hard from taking the stairs three at a time. "Hi, Shannon. Listen . . ."

He heard giggling, realized Charlie was still on the kitchen phone.

"Charlie?"

"Yeah?"

"Get off the phone. Hang up – now."

Silence.

Jack waited for the click, the signal that Charlie had hung up.

"Charlie?"

"Yeah?"

"Get off the phone!"

Charlie giggled, made a rude noise with his lips, then finally hung up.

"Who was that?" Shannon asked.

"My stupid kid brother," Jack said. "He's really rubbish."

"He sounds really cute," she said. "I can't wait to meet him."

Meet him? thought Jack. Why would she ever meet Charlie?

"When are you coming over, baby?" she asked. "I'm kinda lonely."

"I can't come over, Shannon," he said. He decided to be really straight with her.

"What?"

"Listen, I'm, like, really busy. You know, with school and everything. And I've got stuff to do around here for my mum. And a lot of homework to do."

"Didn't you have a good time last night?" she asked, suddenly sounding hurt.

"Of course, I did," he told her. "I had a great time,

Shannon. Really. But . . . but you shouldn't call. I'm very busy now." He took a deep breath. "And I'm not going to be able to go out with you again."

She giggled. "Aw, you're teasing me. Right?"

"No, really. I'm not," he said. "I have to go now. Goodbye, OK? I'll see you at school next week."

He hung up before she could reply.

The receiver was all wet from his hand perspiring. He stood there for a moment, leaning on the desk, waiting for his heart to resume its normal pace, staring at the phone, half expecting it to ring again.

But it remained silent.

Feeling a little better, he headed downstairs to finish his breakfast. Charlie had returned to the cartoons on TV. His mother was unloading the dishwasher. "I thought I'd go over to Walker's. Maybe play some basketball or something," he told her.

She turned around and stared at him, surprised. "Have you forgotten?"

"Huh? Forgotten what?" He picked up a piece of cold toast and chewed it.

"About Charlie's school fair? Remember? You promised to help out?"

"What?" Jack cried. "I did? When did I promise? In my sleep?"

Her expression turned stern. "Come on, Jack. You did promise me. I'm on the PTA, remember. How will it look if you don't show up?"

"But, Mum . . ."

"It isn't anything difficult. Just cloakroom duty. Come on, Jack. You promised."

He hated it when his mother whined like that. But it was starting to come back to him. He had been feeling guilty because he'd promised to take Charlie out bike riding, but then Lauren had come over, and he'd gone off with her instead. And so he'd promised he'd go and help out at Charlie's school fair.

"OK," he said despondently.

What a boring way to spend a Sunday.

His mother smiled. "Good. It should help the time pass for you. When the fair is over, Lauren should be almost home. That's exciting, isn't it?"

"Yeah," he said quietly. He couldn't let on to his mother how pleased he really was that Lauren would be back.

"I'm going to play video games at the fair," Charlie said, coming into the room to get a carton of juice from the fridge.

"You have video games at home," Jack said.

"So?" Charlie hurried back to his cartoons.

A few hours later, Jack was in the noisy, crowded front

hall of Charlie's school, taking coats as parents and kids streamed in for the annual fair. Luckily, it was a clear, dry day, so the coats weren't wet or snow-covered. Across the hall, Mrs Singleton and two other women were selling tickets from large ticket rolls.

"Where's Lauren?" a voice asked.

Jack, weighed down with two long, heavy overcoats, turned to see Mrs Farberson, a friend of his mother's, smiling at him.

"She's in Paris," Jack said. "With her parents. But she's coming home tonight."

"I don't mean to embarrass you," the large, red-faced woman said, handing Jack her fur-collared coat, "but you and Lauren just make the most wonderful couple."

"Thanks," Jack said awkwardly.

"I *am* embarrassing you. I'm sorry," Mrs Farberson said, taking the cloakroom ticket from him. "But you're just so cute together."

Jack smiled, an uncomfortable smile. "Thanks," he said again.

Please go away, he thought.

He hated it when people said that he and Lauren were "cute". This wasn't the first time he had heard it. But he wished it were the last.

"I know your mother is so proud of you," she gushed. She

turned. "Oh – there's your mother over there. I must go and say hello. Bye, Jack. Say hi to Lauren for me."

He watched her make her way through the crowd, then went to hang up her coat.

The rest of the afternoon was uneventful. Only three other people asked him where Lauren was, two of them friends of the DeMarcos, commenting on what a wonderful couple they were.

Jack realized he should have been used to the compliments. He and Lauren had been together since sixth grade, after all. But even though he really was nuts about Lauren, it never failed to embarrass him when people made a fuss about what a terrific couple they were.

It's *our* business – not theirs, he thought.

That evening, he, Charlie, and his mother had just finished dinner, fried chicken and chips from a take-away place down the street. He was about to go upstairs to do some homework, when the phone rang.

"I bet that's Lauren," Mrs Singleton said.

Jack hurried over to the kitchen phone and eagerly grabbed the receiver. "Hello?"

"Hi, baby. Aren't you coming over tonight?" Shannon half talked, half whispered, more of a plea than a question.

60

Jack looked back at his mother, who was staring at him expectantly.

"I'm sorry," he said coldly into the receiver. "We don't need double glazing." He hung up the receiver.

His mother was still staring at him, a thoughtful expression on her face.

"I don't believe those sales people," Jack complained, shaking his head. "They're so rubbish! Can you imagine – calling at dinnertime on Sunday night!"

Why was his mother staring at him like that?

Did she suspect something? Or was he just being paranoid?

He was halfway back to the table when the phone rang again.

Eight

Jack hesitated, staring at the phone on the kitchen wall. It rang again.

"Aren't you going to answer it?" his mother asked impatiently.

"Yeah. I guess." He walked over to it, let it ring a third time, then, with a heavy feeling of dread, picked it up. "Hello?"

"Hi, it's me."

It was Lauren.

"Lauren? Where are you? At home?" he asked, feeling happy – and relieved.

"Yes. I'm home. Totally wrecked. The plane was delayed for over an hour."

"How was it?" Mrs Singleton called from across the room. "Did she have a good time?"

Jack repeated the question. "I had a *great* time!" Lauren exclaimed. "Paris is so beautiful. Like a film set. Not like a real city at all. I just couldn't believe it, couldn't see enough. One day, yesterday I think, I'm too tired to think clearly, we were at Montmartre, looking down from way up high, and it started to snow. This gentle, light snow. It was the most beautiful thing I've ever seen. I don't think I'll ever forget that moment."

"Wow!" Jack said. "Sounds cool!"

"Get down," Lauren said.

"What?"

"Oh. Sorry. I was talking to Fluffernutter. *Get down, you dumb cat.* She won't get off my lap. Jack, I think Fluffernutter missed me more than you did!"

Jack forced a laugh. "That's impossible," he said.

"You missed me?" she asked.

"Of course I did," he said. "It was really rubbish without you around. It just felt so weird."

He couldn't help it. As he said those words, Shannon forced her way into his mind. He thought of Saturday night in Shannon's steamy, dark living room.

"I'm happy to be back, too. I thought about you all the time," Lauren said.

Jack felt so guilty, his words caught in his throat.

"Jack . . . ?"

"Uh . . . listen, Lauren, let's spend all of next weekend together, OK? Just having fun. Just the two of us." He heard the clatter of dishes behind him. His mother was clearing up, noisily loading the dishwasher.

"Jack, have you forgotten? The Junior Chamber of Commerce thing? You know, the Autumn Ball, or whatever they call it?"

"Let's skip it," he urged. He really felt like being with her and no one else. He had to make it up to her for what he had done, for sneaking out with another girl, a girl he had no real interest in.

"We can't skip it, Jack," Lauren said, sighing. "We're being crowned Teens of the Year, remember?"

"So?" he asked, realizing he was sounding just like Charlie.

"So? So they're giving us a cheque," she said.

"Oh. Right. Well," he said, changing his tone, "I'm really looking forward to that!"

She laughed. "Maybe we can sneak out early," she said playfully. "Maybe we'll take the money and run."

"I like the way your mind works," he said.

"Fluffernutter, get down!" she shouted. "Jack, I'd better get off the phone. I'm really tired."

"OK. See you tomorrow at school," he said, not wanting to hang up.

"Yeah. See you tomorrow," she said softly, and then added, "I missed you."

"Me, too," he said and hung up feeling very guilty.

"Did they have a good time?" Mrs Singleton asked, struggling to close the dishwasher. The handle always stuck.

Jack hurried over to help her. "Yeah. She said it was great. It snowed one day."

"In Paris? That must have been beautiful," she said dreamily. "I've always wanted to see Paris in the snow."

Jack's mother had never been abroad. With the two boys to bring up, there was never enough money.

"Well, I'm glad they made it back OK," she said, giving the worktop a final wipe.

Jack suddenly had the urge to get out of the house, to get into the car, to drive somewhere fast, to drive anywhere, to just get away. "I'm going out for a short while," he told his mother, avoiding her glance.

"Are you going to Lauren's?"

"No. She's too tired. I'm just going for a drive, maybe stop at Walker's," he said, heading to the cupboard for his jacket.

"On a Sunday night? Don't you have homework?"

"I'll be back soon," he said impatiently.

"Do what you want." She disappeared up the stairs.

Jack pulled on his jacket and searched the shelf for his Raiders cap. Rummaging through the scarves and gloves and woollen ski hats, he couldn't find it.

My cap. Where could it be?

And then he realized. He had left it at Shannon's.

Yes. She had tossed it across the room, and he had never retrieved it.

Maybe I should drive over there and get it, he thought, stepping out through the door into a blustery, cold night. It *is* my favourite cap, after all.

I'll just knock on the door. Stay on the front porch. Ask for my cap.

No way, he told himself.

No way I'm going back to Shannon's. I'm never going back there. Never.

It was a promise he was making to himself, a solemn promise, to him – and to Lauren.

Never.

She can keep the hat.

He climbed into the old Ford and drove aimlessly around town for nearly an hour. Houses and shops whirred by in the darkness as a light fog settled in. Jack paid no attention to where he was or where he was going. He felt like driving, just driving.

He didn't think about anything. The darkness, the cold air, the wisps of soft, grey fog all calmed him. By the time he returned home and pulled the car into the garage, he was feeling very relaxed.

The next morning, he arrived at school early, a little past seven-thirty, and found Shannon waiting for him at his locker.

Nine

J ack stopped short, several metres away. "Shannon?" His voice echoed in the empty corridor.

A warm smile spread across her face. She didn't wait for him to come closer. She ran up to him and jumped up to give him a playful kiss on the cheek.

"Surprised?"

"Yeah," he said, taking a step back. He pulled off his school bag and let it slide to the floor.

She was wearing a bright red jumper that clashed with her red hair, and tight black jeans. Stepping forward quickly, she tilted her head up for another kiss.

"Whoa. Stop," he said sharply.

"It's OK, baby," she replied softly. "It's nice and early. There's no one around."

"Shannon – what are you *doing* here?" Jack demanded.

"I wanted to see you," she said, tossing her long hair back over one shoulder. "You're my baby now."

"No, I'm not," he said angrily. He picked up his bag and slammed it against the wall. "Stop saying that."

Her dark eyes narrowed. "You liked it on Saturday night," she said. She looked like she was about to cry.

She's a good actress, he thought.

It made him even angrier.

"Saturday night was great," he told her. "But it was just one date, OK? It was great. But that's it. We can't go out. OK? We can't."

"But, baby—"

"Shannon – please!" He looked behind him. A few kids were wandering into the building. Lockers were being opened. Voices echoed down the long corridor. "I'm going out with someone," he told her. "Someone I'm very serious about. She's very important to me and—"

"Hey, man – how's it going?"

A hand grabbed Jack's shoulder from behind.

Jack wheeled around to see Walker grinning down at him. "Where were you yesterday afternoon?" Walker asked. "I called round at your house and . . ."

Walker stopped because he noticed Shannon. "Oh," he said, seeing the desperate expression on Shannon's face and realizing that he had interrupted a conversation. "Sorry, man. I didn't know . . ."

Walker's face filled with embarrassment. Waving his big hand at Jack, he started to back down the hallway.

"No, Walker – wait!" Jack said. "Wait!" He picked up his bag.

"I've got to go," Walker shouted, still looking embarrassed, and disappeared around the corner.

Shannon stepped in front of Jack, blocking his way. The hall was crowded now. Jack looked towards the doors, expecting to see Lauren come walking in.

"You're not being nice to me, baby," Shannon said, putting a hand gently on the front of Jack's jacket.

"Shannon, give me a break—"

"I was so nice to you," she said softly, ignoring his anger, not moving her hand from his chest. "But you're not being nice to me." A tear formed in the corner of each eye.

The bell rang.

She lifted her hand off the front of his jacket. The single tears were rolling down her pale cheeks. She turned quickly and ran.

He stared after her, watching her run through the crowded hall, her hair flowing wildly behind her. A few seconds later, she turned the corner and disappeared from view.

Maybe I finally got through to her, he thought. Maybe she finally gets the picture.

Feeling a lot better, he unlocked his locker and got ready to start the school day.

*

"Shouldn't I get my coat?" Lauren asked.

"No. It isn't that cold out. Really," Jack urged. "You'll see."

She followed him through the door and onto the lawn behind the school. They were both carrying their lunchboxes. It was Jack's idea to eat their lunch outside, not only for the fresh air but for the privacy.

"It feels like you've been gone a lot longer than a week," he said, sitting down under a large maple tree, bare and wintery-looking. He patted the leafy ground beside him. Lauren sat down.

"You're just saying that to be sweet," she said, affectionately pressing her forehead against his cheek.

"Yeah, you're right," he said, and laughed, casually putting an arm around her shoulders.

It was so easy being with Lauren, he realized. So comfortable. So *right*.

"What have you got?" Lauren asked, removing his arm so she could open her lunchbox.

"Ham and cheese, I think. Every day it's ham and cheese. So boring."

"Well, who makes your lunch?" she asked.

"I do!"

They both laughed.

"It's not too cold out here. You were right," she said,

unwrapping her tuna fish sandwich. Half the tuna fish fell out onto her lap.

"Smooth move," Jack said.

"The food was a little better in Paris," Lauren said, picking up a clump of tuna with her hand and putting it into her mouth. "The bread. The bread was the most spectacular thing. I could just live on the bread. It was so good!"

"Better than Hovis?" Jack joked.

"Hey, Jack?" Lauren's tone suddenly changed.

"Yeah?" he asked, with a mouth full of sandwich.

"Who's that girl?"

"What?"

Lauren pointed.

Jack looked up to see Shannon standing on the path a few yards away. Her jacket was open, and she had her hands on her hips as she stared intently at Jack and Lauren.

"Why is she looking at us like that?" Lauren asked.

"I don't know," Jack told her. "I've never seen her before."

Ten

Jack walked home after school, thinking about Shannon. The sky had turned grey and threatening. Gusting winds tossed waves of dead, brown leaves at his feet, but he stepped through them without noticing.

Shannon, what am I going to do about you? he thought.

How can I get through to you?

It had been so embarrassing at lunch. Shannon had stood there like a statue, staring angrily at Jack and Lauren for the longest time. What did she think I would do? Jack asked himself. Go running over to her and invite her to join us?

Why can't she take a hint?

I've been straight with her. I've told her exactly how I feel. What more can I do?

He turned the corner onto his street and saw Shannon sitting on his front steps.

Oh, man.

Now what?

She hadn't seen him yet. She was sitting with her head down, her knees tucked between her hands. His first impulse was to turn and run in the other direction.

But that wouldn't do any good, he realized. She'd be sitting there when his mother got home with Charlie. And how would he ever explain Shannon to his mother?

No. He had to face her. He had to make her understand that she had to leave him alone.

He took a deep breath and, with long, determined strides, walked over the leaf-strewn lawn to the front porch. "Hi, Shannon," he said wearily, letting his expression show how unhappy he was to see her.

"You have to break up with her," Shannon said, raising her head slowly. Her eyes were red-rimmed, as if she'd been crying. Her hair was more tangled than usual, a twisted strand falling down over one eye.

"What? Are you crazy?"

She didn't react to him at all, didn't even look at him. "You have to break up with her," she repeated in a low, steady voice.

"Shannon, there's no way I'm breaking up with Lauren," Jack said, standing over her, shifting his weight uncomfortably. He pulled off his school bag and heaved it onto the path. "No way."

"But you're *my* baby now." She tugged at the strand of hair, but didn't push it away from her face.

"No. I'm not," Jack said firmly. "I'm not! D'you hear me? I'm *not*!" He held himself back. He could feel his anger taking over, feel it turn to rage. He felt himself getting out of control.

Why didn't she listen to him? Why was she doing this to him?

He wanted to hit something. He wanted to hit *her*.

He closed his fists, then opened them again.

Get control, get control, get control, he repeated to himself.

"I'm not good enough for you?" she asked, looking up at him, staring into his eyes with her big, brown, sad eyes. "Is that it?"

"No, that's not it," he said coldly. "We had one date. Now it's over. I've already told you." He looked down the street, afraid he might see the Ford heading home with Charlie and his mother.

"You're hurting my feelings," Shannon wailed, tears running down her puffy cheeks. "You're hurting my feelings, Jack. I'm getting very upset."

"Don't be upset," he said, feeling helpless, nervously watching the street. "It was just *one* date, Shannon. Be fair – OK?"

"My brothers won't like this," she said, wiping her wet cheeks with her hand.

"What?"

"My brothers," she said, sniffling. "They don't like it when people aren't nice to me."

She's threatening me, Jack thought angrily. I don't believe this. She's threatening me with her three monster brothers.

"I'm trying to be nice to you," he said. "I'm trying to be honest. OK? I think you should forget about me. I think . . ."

He stopped. He saw his mum's car turn the corner, Charlie beside her in the front seat.

"Listen, Shannon – you've got to go – *now*." He grabbed her arms and pulled her to her feet.

"Let go of me!" she cried, struggling away from him.

"My mum is almost here," he said frantically. "You've got to go."

"But I want to meet Mum," she insisted, following Jack's gaze to the street. "I think it's time I met Mum, don't you?"

"No!" The car was halfway down the street. "Listen, Shannon – go now and I'll call you tonight," he offered, tugging at the sleeve of her jacket.

"Huh? Really?" Her whole face brightened.

"Yeah. I'll call you. After dinner. We'll have a long talk," he said. "Just go. Now. Please!"

"OK, baby. Call me tonight," she said, smiling for the first time. She started towards the driveway, but he grabbed her and pulled her the other way, to the side of the house.

"Go that way. Call you tonight. Promise," he said.

She ran off, stopping once to look back at him uncertainly, then disappeared through the hedges to the street just as his mum's car pulled up the driveway.

"AAAAAAGH!" Jack screamed, letting out only a little of his anger and frustration.

What am I going to *do*?

Furiously, he picked up his bag and heaved it towards the front door. He hadn't meant to throw it as hard as he did. It crashed into the storm door, shattering the glass.

"No!" he screamed. "Oh, no!"

He could hear the car doors slam around the back, could hear Charlie's high-pitched voice repeating, "I'm hungry! I'm hungry!"

Jack started trudging up the driveway to join them when something caught his eye. A shadow. A large one. Moving quickly from the side of the house, along the hedges towards the street.

"Hey . . ." Jack called out.

He saw a man, a very large man, wearing a long raincoat, appear between the hedges, then quickly duck out of view.

"Hey . . ." Jack called again, at first not believing his eyes.

He stood frozen on the driveway, more surprised than frightened, staring at the hedges that were now still.

Someone was here, Jack thought.

Someone was watching Shannon and me.

And then he realized. It must have been one of Shannon's brothers. "My brothers are enormous," she had told him, and this guy, even seen from behind, seen in a split second, was certainly enormous, his coat billowing behind him as he ran.

"My brothers don't like it when people aren't nice to me," Shannon had said. It was definitely meant as a threat. And one of the three hulks had been standing there the whole time, standing in the shadows at the side of the house, watching, listening.

Maybe the whole family is crazy, Jack thought, chilled by the thought.

What am I going to do?

Trying to conceal his troubled feelings, he hurried around to the back where his mother was struggling with the back door, several shopping bags in her hands. "Jack," she called out, "are you just getting home?"

"Yeah," he lied. He was getting used to lying.

"I'm hungry," Charlie whined.

"I know, I know," Mrs Singleton groaned.

"The front door is broken," Jack said. "The glass on the storm door, it's shattered."

"What?" His mother's mouth dropped open. "How?"

Jack shrugged. "I don't know. I saw it as I came up the drive. Looks like somebody threw something at it."

"Well, maybe we'll just remove it or put the screen back up," she said, frowning. "I can't afford a new storm door." She brightened and held up the shopping bags. "Especially after the money I spent on this."

"What's that?" Jack asked.

"I'm hungry," Charlie shouted.

She pushed open the door, and they went inside. "It's the new dress I bought for Saturday. You know. For the Junior Chamber of Commerce."

"You bought a special dress for that?" Jack asked. He started to open the fridge, but Charlie got there first, darting between his legs to win the race.

"Of course," his mother said, smiling as she held up the silky dress to show him. "It's a special day, isn't it? I had to buy the perfect dress in honour of the perfect couple. I'm just so proud of you and Lauren. Everyone is."

"I'm not," Charlie said. "I'm hungry."

In his room after dinner, Jack tried to concentrate on his history textbook. But he couldn't read an entire paragraph without thinking about Shannon. And about her brother, spying on them.

Slamming the book shut in exasperation, he reached for the phone. I'm going to call Shannon, he decided, and tell her once and for all that I don't want to go out with her again, that I don't want her to ever call me again.

But then he pulled his hand back. No. I've already told her. A hundred times. I promised to call her tonight. But I'm not going to. And when she sees that I'm not calling, she'll realize that I'm serious.

And then her enormous brother will beat me to a pulp, he thought.

He stared at the phone. No. No way. I'm not going to call her.

He opened the textbook again and shuffled through to find his place. He still hadn't found it when the phone rang.

He felt his heart skip a beat. He jumped to his feet.

It rang a second time. A third.

He didn't want to pick it up, but no one downstairs seemed to be answering it. "Hello?" he said softly, timidly.

"Where were you, man?" a familiar voice asked without any greeting.

"Walker?"

"Yeah, it's me. Where were you?"

Jack was so relieved to hear Walker's voice, he could barely hear what his friend was saying. "What do you mean?"

"Where were you? Why weren't you at practice?" Walker asked impatiently.

"Oh, no!" Jack slapped his forehead. He had been so obsessed with Shannon that he'd forgot all about his after-school football practice.

"Coach Hawkins was really steamed," Walker said. "He gave Berman extra time. Had him passing all afternoon."

Berman was the second-string quarterback. He wasn't bad. Jack knew if he slipped up, Berman would take his place in an instant.

"Tell me Berman wasn't any good," Jack pleaded.

"He wasn't bad," Walker said. "He's really got an arm. He can heave the ball a mile. I think Hawkins was impressed."

"You're a real pal," Jack said sarcastically. "I *asked* you to tell me he wasn't any good!"

"So where were you?" Walker asked.

"I was . . . busy," Jack said, struggling unsuccessfully to think of a good excuse. "I had to do some things . . . for my mum."

There was a long silence at the other end. Jack knew that Walker wasn't buying his story.

"You've been acting kind of weird lately," Walker said finally. "Who was that girl you were talking to?"

"Girl?"

"Yeah. You know. Really small. With the wild, red hair."

"Oh. I don't know her name. She has a locker next to mine, that's all," Jack told him.

I'm lying to everyone now, he thought.

He had a sudden strong urge to tell Walker everything, but held back. Walker would just make a joke, Jack thought. Or he might tell someone else. I've got to handle this on my own.

He knew he couldn't take a chance. What if word somehow got back to Lauren?

"Are you sure everything's OK?" Walker asked.

"Yeah. Fine," Jack said. "See you tomorrow, man."

He hung up and reached for the textbook. "How am I ever going to read this?" he asked himself aloud.

The phone rang again.

Walker almost always called back with something he'd forgotten. Jack picked up the receiver. "Hello?"

"Baby, you didn't call." Shannon's whispery voice reverberated in his ear. He could feel his neck muscles tighten.

His entire body tensed. He couldn't hold back his anger any longer. "I didn't call you – and I'm *never* going to call you!" he screamed.

He could hear a sharp intake of breath followed by a low whimper on the other end. He didn't care if he hurt her now. He was too angry to care.

"I don't *want* to call you, Shannon!" he cried. "I don't

want to *see* you! We're not going out. Not ever. Hear? I don't want to go out with you."

He took a breath. His heart was pounding. His mouth was dry. There was no sound at all on the other end of the line.

"Leave me alone," he continued. "I mean it. Leave me alone, Shannon. Don't call me again." He slammed the receiver down without waiting for any kind of reply.

"There," he said aloud and reached for his textbook. "That's done."

Eleven

Jack felt good the next morning, having slept well, a peaceful, dreamless sleep. Lauren called while he was eating breakfast. He was happy to hear her voice.

"I've been thinking about your birthday," she said.

"Huh?" He swallowed a mouthful of Frosted Flakes. "My birthday is two weeks away."

"So? How shall we celebrate?" she asked. "Should we have a party or something?"

"A party? No. I . . ." He realized he wasn't awake enough to discuss this. "Can we talk about it later?"

Lauren always did this to him. She couldn't bear to be thinking about something alone. If she had something on her mind, she had to call no matter what time it was and make him think about it, too.

"D'you want to meet after school?" she asked.

"No. I've got football practice," he said. A heavy feeling of dread sank through his body. He knew he was going to get yelled at by Coach Hawkins this afternoon for missing practice. "How about lunch?"

"OK," she agreed. "The usual place. And think about your birthday, OK?"

"OK," he said, and hung up. He gulped down the last spoonful of the sweet cereal, tilted the bowl to his mouth to drink the milk, then started to look for Charlie. "Charlie – where are you? We're going to be late."

Charlie came limping into the room, one trainer on, one off. "I've got a knot in my shoelace," he whined, handing the shoe to Jack.

How does he do it? Jack wondered, shaking his head. How does he get a knot in his shoelace *every* morning?

Jack dropped Charlie off at the elementary school, then continued on to the high school a couple of streets away. When he turned the corner and started down the corridor to his locker, he was relieved to see that Shannon wasn't waiting for him there.

He smiled, feeling better, feeling the sense of dread begin to lift. He locked up his jacket, then, carrying the books he'd need that morning, talked with friends until the bell rang. Shannon was nowhere to be seen.

After the fourth lesson, he met Lauren at their usual

meeting place outside the canteen. "You've had your hair cut!" he exclaimed, immediately noticing her new, short hair.

"Do you like it?" she asked, patting it in exaggerated fashion like a primping film star. "I wanted to look nice for Saturday."

"Are we really going to show up for that thing on Saturday?" he asked, rolling his eyes.

"No. You're going to turn down the money," she replied dryly. "What do you need money for?"

"OK, OK. We're doing it," he said. "But it's going to be so rubbish."

"It's only a few hours of your life, Jack," Lauren said, pulling him into the canteen. "What could be so terrible?"

As they ate their sandwiches, Jack kept alert, looking for Shannon. But she never appeared.

He didn't see her all day. Driving home after football practice, he wondered if she'd be waiting for him on the front porch.

The afternoon was warm for November, but grey clouds were rolling in, bringing a chill to the air. The bare trees seemed to shiver along the sides of the street as he turned onto his street and then pulled up the drive.

He glanced at the front porch then moved his eyes around the front garden.

No Shannon. She wasn't there.

"All right!" he shouted happily inside the car.

He jumped out of the car and stretched. He suddenly felt very light, as if a heavy weight had been lifted from him.

Finally.

I finally made her understand.

Carrying his school bag by the straps, he walked towards the back door. But he stopped on the path, suddenly remembering Ernie, his snake, and lowered the bag to the ground.

I'd better check on Ernie, he thought. I forgot all about him yesterday.

Walking quickly, he headed to the side of the garage. Two fat, grey squirrels scampered along the fence at the back of the garden, kicking up the dead leaves as they ran.

When the cage came into view, Jack stopped.

And gaped.

The top of the screened cage was off, lying on the ground.

Had Ernie escaped?

Jack started to run. How had the top come off? It was too heavy to be blown off by the wind. Someone had to have *taken* it off.

But – wait. The snake hadn't escaped. It was still in the cage.

Yes. As Jack came up to it, he could see Ernie on the glass cage floor.

"Ernie, what's . . ." Jack started to say. But his mouth dropped open in horror, and he never finished his greeting.

The snake, he saw, had been cut in two.

Twelve

"You have to break up with her, baby."

Shannon called him right after dinner. He was upstairs, pacing back and forth in his room, unable to get the picture of his pet snake out of his mind. Ernie had been sliced cleanly across the middle, cut into two almost perfect halves.

Jack was standing right next to the phone when it rang. Startled, he uttered a short cry, then picked up the receiver before the first ring had ended. "Hello?"

"You have to break up with her, baby."

Shannon didn't even bother to say hello. Her voice was as whispery as ever, but there was a hard, determined tone to it, an edge Jack had never heard before.

"Shannon – did you kill my snake?" he asked angrily, balling his free hand into a tight fist.

"You have to break up with her. You *have* to."

"Did you? Did you kill my snake? Answer me!"

"You have to break up with her, Jack."

Jack made the fist tighter and tighter until his hand ached with pain. Slowly, he relaxed his hand. His voice trembled from anger as he spoke. "Stop repeating that and answer my question."

"You've hurt me, baby," she said, her little-girl voice returning. "Please don't make me hurt you again."

"Again? What do you mean by *again*, Shannon?" he screamed. "You're admitting it? You're admitting that you did it?"

"Come over tonight, and we'll talk about it," she whispered.

"What? Are you serious . . . ?"

"Come over," she repeated playfully. "There's no one here but me. I'm very lonely, baby."

"Shannon – I – I'm going to call the police," he said, surprising himself. He didn't know if he was serious or not. He hadn't really thought about it. The words just popped out.

"The police?" her voice grew even tinier. Then, to his surprise, she giggled. "My brothers wouldn't like that."

"I don't care about your brothers," he declared. "I've decided. I'm calling the police."

There was a pause. Then she said softly, "No, you're not. Because then Lauren would find out. Wouldn't she? And her parents. I'd have to tell everyone then, wouldn't I? Everyone would know about you and me, baby."

"Now, wait . . ." He didn't know what to say next. Shannon was right, of course. There was no way he could go to the police. If Lauren found out, she'd break up with him. He'd lose her. He'd lose . . . everything.

Besides, he had no way of proving that Shannon killed the snake. The police would laugh at him, wouldn't listen to him at all.

"Come over, baby," she urged. "Stop being so silly."

"I'm never coming over," he said slowly, speaking each word clearly and distinctly. "Hear me? I'm never coming over. And if you call me, or threaten me, or do something else to me – *anything* – I'll call the police, Shannon. I really will."

He hung up the phone and realized he was trembling all over.

A loud knock on the bedroom door made him jump.

The door swung open, and Charlie came skipping in, a big grin on his face. "What do you want?" Jack snapped, not meaning to sound so harsh, trying to calm down, not wanting Charlie to see how upset he was.

"Can I ask you a favour?" Charlie asked, fiddling with the homework papers on Jack's desk.

"Yeah. I guess."

"It's a pretty big favour," Charlie said.

"That's OK. Go ahead and ask."

"It's kind of a *really* big favour," Charlie said reluctantly.

"Charlie . . ." Jack snapped angrily.

"Could I borrow Ernie?" Charlie asked. "We're having a science show-and-tell, and I told everyone I was bringing a snake."

"No. Sorry," Jack said quickly. He pictured the snake, lying so still and straight, cut into two halves, its insides pouring out onto the glass cage floor.

"Why not?" Charlie asked angrily, shoving Jack's papers across the desk.

"Ernie escaped," Jack said, thinking quickly. "I . . . uh . . . didn't get a chance to tell you."

"He escaped?" Charlie stared up at him, his face filled with surprise.

"Yeah. The lid came off somehow. It was off when I came home, and Ernie was gone."

Actually, Jack had lifted the two snake halves into a plastic bag and buried the bag behind the garage.

"You mean, Ernie is out in the back garden somewhere?" Charlie asked, looking upset.

"I don't think so," Jack told him, putting a reassuring hand on his shoulder. "I searched all over for him. I think he probably went to the woods. Snakes like it in the woods."

Charlie wanted to talk about it more, but Jack had

homework to do and guided him out of the room. That night, Jack couldn't get to sleep. The picture of his pet, sliced so neatly, so coldly, so cruelly, wouldn't fade from his mind.

It was already dark when football practice ended the next afternoon. The sky was inky black with eerie grey streaks of clouds, ghostly images floating low overhead. The air was cold and damp.

"It could snow for the Madison game on Friday night," Jack said, zipping his jacket up to the top, ducking his head into the collar for protection against the damp wind.

Walker pulled his Hard Rock Café cap low on his forehead as he loped along beside Jack. His glasses reflected the light from a street lamp. "I guess snow would help us and hurt them," he said thoughtfully.

"How come?" Jack asked.

Walker shrugged. "No reason. Just trying to sound as if I know something." He laughed. Jack punched him on the shoulder.

They turned the corner onto Jack's street. The wind seemed to blow into their faces no matter which direction they walked. Despite the cold, Walker had his jacket unzipped.

"What are you and Lauren doing after the game?" Walker asked.

"I don't know," Jack replied. "D'you think Hawkins will get off my case before Friday?"

"You know Hawkins," Walker said. "He thinks it's good psychology to make you angry. Thinks it gets you fired up."

"It only gets me angry," Jack said. "I didn't play so badly today."

As they reached the corner, Walker pretended to walk right into the postbox. He hit the postbox hard with his whole body and fell back onto the pavement. Walker was always doing things like that, walking into trees, falling down. It usually cracked Jack up, but he didn't feel like laughing today.

Jack helped Walker up. "I hope you throw better blocks than that on Friday night," he said.

He looked up and saw Shannon standing on the pavement in front of them. The streetlight above cast her in an eerie green glow. She was wearing the same green jacket. Her jeans were tucked into knee-high black boots. In the pale light, she looked frail and tiny, old-fashioned-looking with her long hair flowing freely behind her shoulders, like a Victorian painting of an angel.

"Hi, Jack," she said softly, smiling with pleasure at the shock on his face.

"Shannon, I warned you . . ." Jack said, looking at Walker, who was staring wide-eyed at Shannon and nervously re-adjusting his cap.

"Why didn't you come to see me last night?" Shannon asked, still smiling, stepping closer.

Jack didn't reply. He could feel his muscles tense. He was too angry to be embarrassed, but he wished Walker weren't there.

"Hi," Walker said to Shannon. "I'm Jack's good-looking friend. David Walker. But you can call me Walker like everyone else."

Shannon didn't look at Walker, didn't acknowledge that he was there. "You hurt my feelings, baby," she said to Jack in her little-girl voice. "Why didn't you come over?"

Jack's face was frozen in anger. He refused to reply, hoping his silence would force her to retreat, to disappear.

"Hey . . . if you two want to be alone . . ." Walker said, casting a meaningful look at Jack.

"No," Jack replied quickly. "Let's go, man. I don't know this girl."

"She seems to know you – *baby*!" Walker cracked. He smiled at Shannon, who continued to ignore him.

"Why won't you be nice to me, Jack?" Shannon asked, her tiny voice barely carrying over the wind. "I was very nice to you. Remember?"

"Wow!" Walker exclaimed.

"Let's go, man," Jack said, avoiding Shannon's stare.

He started to walk past her, but she stepped into his path, blocking his way. "Don't go, Jack."

Still ignoring her, he pulled to the right, walking fast. "Let's go, Walker," he insisted.

But Shannon grabbed his arm with both hands, as if making a high shoulder tackle. "Wait, baby."

"Hey – let go!" Jack protested.

Shannon slid her hands down the sleeve of Jack's jacket and squeezed his hand between hers. Jack saw Walker behind them, staring in disbelief. He tried to pull his hand away from her, but her grip was surprisingly strong.

"Don't go, baby," she pleaded, tears running down her cheeks.

"Come on, Shannon – let go of me!" Jack cried.

"You two want to wrestle?" Walker suggested. "How about two out of three? I'm betting on *her*!"

"Let go. I don't want to hold hands!" Jack yelled, surprised by how strong this frail-looking little girl was.

"Don't go. Please – stay with me!" Tears were streaming down her face. "Don't make me hurt you, Jack. I don't want to hurt you."

As she said this, she grabbed two of his fingers with one hand, the other two fingers with her other hand.

"Hey . . . !" Jack cried, struggling to free himself.

But she was so strong, so surprisingly strong.

And then, her face distorted with fury, Shannon pulled down hard, yanking the fingers in two different directions.

At first, Jack didn't feel anything.

He heard the loud *crack*.

It was loud enough for all three of them to hear it.

He screamed as the pain coursed up his arm, then shot through his entire body. Everything went red, then white. He dropped to his knees. He had never felt such pain. His entire right side throbbed. Gasping for breath, he held his arm close to his body, as if trying to protect it, to squeeze away the pain.

When Jack focused again, he saw Walker, looking pale, his mouth open, gulping air, his eyes wide behind the black-framed glasses, gaping at Shannon with shock and disbelief.

Shannon had stepped back under the eerie green light of the street lamp. She seemed to be shocked by what she had done. Wet tears slid down her cheeks. She tugged at the sides of her hair with both hands.

"Shannon – my hand . . ." Jack managed to cry out in a terrified voice he didn't recognize. He held the injured hand up by the wrist with his left hand.

"I'm so sorry, baby," she cried, shaking her head. "I'm so, so sorry." Then she turned and ran, her jacket flapping behind her.

"My hand . . ." Jack called after her. He looked round at Walker. "It's – it's broken!"

Thirteen

Behind him in the stands, Glenview fans cheered and shouted. Jack leaned forward on the bench to get a better view. On the first play from scrimmage, Berman went back to pass. He looked left, then right.

Too long. You're taking too long, Jack thought. You're going to eat the ball.

He was right. Berman was swarmed by three gold-and-green-uniformed Madison players. He hit the ground hard, sacked, and they piled on top of him.

The crowd in the stands groaned and then grew quiet.

Jack turned downfield to see the cheerleaders. They were facing the crowd, clapping in rhythm, shouting a "Go, Tigers" cheer. Lauren stood in the centre, leaping high in her short, green-and-white-skirted cheerleader uniform. She looks great, Jack thought.

Shifting the heavy cast on his hand, he turned back to the

game in time to see a handoff to Barker, stopped at the line of scrimmage. Third down. The Madison players seemed really fired-up. A cheer went up from the Madison supporters on the other side of the field.

Jack groaned as the next play began, and Berman fumbled the snap from centre. Luckily a Glenview player fell on the ball. But now it was fourth down. The Tigers had to punt.

I should be in there, Jack thought, pounding his knee with the heavy, white cast over his hand. He looked down at the cast, feeling his anger starting to rise.

But he realized he was more angry with himself than with Shannon. I let everyone down, he thought. I let Coach Hawkins down. I let the team down.

He looked past the bench towards the cheerleaders. Lauren had turned around to watch the punt. Her short hair glowed golden under the bright white stadium lights. She turned and looked back at him, her smile momentarily fading. Their eyes met. He waved at her with the cast. She turned back to the field.

I let Lauren down, too, Jack thought dejectedly. And her parents. And everyone else who believes in me.

The punt was short. The Glenview supporters behind the team bench groaned. Madison would be starting out on the Glenview forty-five.

"Dee-fence! Dee-fence!" the cheerleaders were chanting.

After Shannon broke Jack's hand, Walker had taken him to casualty at Glenview General. On the way, Jack had to explain a little bit about Shannon, after first making Walker swear to total secrecy.

"She's been after me for weeks," he lied, feeling bad, feeling guilty about all the lying he'd had to do. But what choice did he have? "She calls me, and comes to my house, and follows me everywhere," he told Walker. "She wants me to go out with her, but of course I won't. She's crazy. Just plain crazy."

"You've got to call the police," Walker urged.

"No, I can't," Jack said, resting his head on the seat in Walker's car, grimacing as his hand throbbed with pain. "The police won't do anything."

"But she broke your hand, man!" Walker exclaimed, nearly driving through a red light. "That's assault, isn't it?"

"She'd just say it was an accident," Jack said softly, afraid to tell Walker the real reason he didn't want to call the police. Afraid to tell Walker any of the real story.

"Well, at least you can call her parents," Walker suggested, turning into the hospital driveway. "Let them know what their daughter is doing. Tell them she's got to be put on a leash or something."

"Yeah. That's a good idea," Jack had said thoughtfully.

Walker was right, he realized. He *could* call Shannon's parents and tell them that Shannon was driving him crazy. Or maybe even talk to one of her brothers.

The whole family couldn't be as weird as she is – could they?

He told everyone, including his mother, that he had slammed his hand in a car door. Lauren had been terribly sympathetic. She called him a clumsy idiot, but she said it in a nice way. Coach Hawkins hadn't been as nice.

That night, trying to get to sleep, Jack kept hearing the crack his fingers had made as Shannon pulled them in different directions. The pain had subsided, but his hand itched constantly, and of course, he couldn't scratch it.

The next morning, he tried calling her house at lunchtime, hoping to catch someone at home while Shannon was at school. He had carefully rehearsed what he was going to say, repeating it endlessly in his mind. He was going to tell them that he was a friend of Shannon's and that as a friend, he was calling to say that she needed help, that he was very worried about her. He was going to tell them that she had been calling him constantly, following him around, and threatening violence.

It was the truth, after all.

If they weren't sympathetic, he was going to threaten to call the police. He hoped he wouldn't have to do that. He wanted to stop Shannon. But he didn't want to get her so upset that she'd do something drastic, like call Lauren.

Despite his endless rehearsal of what he was going to say, his heart was pounding as he punched in her phone number. The phone rang and rang, but no one answered.

He tried again right after school. Again, there was no one at home.

That night, he dialled her house again, hoping that one of her parents or brothers would answer. But he immediately recognized Shannon's breathy "Hello?" and slammed down the phone.

Her "hello" had sounded so eager, so hopeful, that for a moment Jack had felt sorry for her. But then he glanced at his hand in the big, white cast and remembered that the football season was over for him, as were his chances of being named player of the year, and he felt only anger.

He tried calling three more times during the week. But Shannon had answered each time, and each time he had immediately hung up. Finally he gave up the idea, and his carefully rehearsed speech faded from his mind.

Now, here he was on Friday night, sitting on the team bench in his hoody and jeans, balancing his heavy cast on his lap, feeling terribly guilty and terribly sorry for himself at the same time, watching the Tigers lose to a team he knew he could have beaten.

The final score was 21–3.

As the team trudged to the locker room, Jack stayed on the bench, slumping low, feeling chilled by the night air, staring across the now-empty field as people made their way out of the stadium.

"Hey, man, we missed you," Walker said, standing over Jack, his helmet in his hand, his hair matted down on his head, sweat covering his forehead despite the cold night air.

"Yeah, well . . ." Jack stared across the field uncomfortably.

"Only one more game," Walker said, breathing hard. "That girl still bothering you?"

"No," Jack told him, still avoiding his glance. "I haven't seen her all week."

"Hey – that's great!" Walker said. "That's terrific."

"You haven't told anyone about her?" Jack asked nervously.

"No. No way," Walker replied, looking hurt that Jack would ask that question. "You meeting Lauren?"

"Yeah. She's getting changed. Then we're going to get something to eat. Want to come?"

"No. Thanks. I'm going to hang out with some of the guys on the team. Later, OK? I've got to get changed." He jogged off towards the locker room.

Jack stayed on the bench for a while, staring at the shiny green turf, thinking about Shannon and about Lauren. He was startled when the stadium lights went out, casting everything in darkness.

Standing up, he turned to see Lauren watching him from the track at the edge of the field. "Hi," she called, waving. She had changed into jeans. Her coat was open, revealing a white jumper. "What on earth are you doing?"

"Nothing much," he said, hurrying over to her. "Just waiting for you."

"You were sitting there feeling sorry for yourself," she said, taking his arm and giving him a quick kiss on the cheek. Her nose and lips felt hot against his cold face. "Admit it."

"Maybe a little," he confessed, smiling guiltily.

"Well, I have some news that should cheer you up," she said, holding tightly onto his arm as they walked to the carpark.

"The Junior Chamber of Commerce has disbanded, and we don't have to go to that stupid thing tomorrow?" he joked.

She slapped his arm, accidentally hitting the top of the cast. "Oh. Sorry. No. My news is that Dad has decided to take on an intern for the summer at his firm, and you're it."

"Huh?"

"You heard me, Jack. You can work as an intern there this summer, and he'll even pay you. Not a lot, but it'll give you some spending money for when we're at Princeton in the autumn."

"Wow! That's great!" Jack exclaimed, brightening.

"Am I cheering you up?" she asked, clinging to him, pulling the coat together with her free hand.

"Yeah. You're doing a great job," Jack said sincerely.

"Well, here's more," she said, grinning at him. "Dad says you can come up to Cape Cod with us in August and stay for two whole weeks."

Jack stopped and turned to her. "Really?" He hadn't been looking forward to August. He knew Lauren would spend the whole month up at the Cape with her family, and he wouldn't get to see her. "That's awesome!" he declared.

"Stick with me, kid," she said playfully. "I'll show you a good time."

"August is a long way away," he complained. "It's only November."

"Hey – I'm trying to cheer you up," she said, laughing. "Give me a break."

"Please – don't say *break*," he groaned, holding up his cast.

She gave him a playful shove. He reached for her, but then stopped short as the car-park came into view.

There, leaning casually against the bonnet of his Ford, was Shannon. She was wearing the same clothes as the last time he'd seen her – jeans tucked into high black boots, the green jacket, which she always seemed to wear no matter how cold it was.

Had she seen him?

No. Not yet. She was looking towards the other stadium exit.

Looking past her, trying to decide what to do, Jack's eyes bulged in surprise. Someone else was standing a few cars down, hiding in the shadows, keeping low behind a black Jeep.

It was the large man Jack had seen running along the hedges from his garden. Shannon's enormous brother!

A wave of fear shot through him. Why had Shannon brought her brother? Why was he hiding in the shadows a few cars away from Shannon?

She had already broken his hand. Wasn't that enough? Now what did she and her huge brother have planned for him?

"Uh . . . can we take your car?" Jack asked Lauren, trying to make his voice sound normal.

Lauren looked at him, confused. "Huh? Why?"

"Uh . . . mine doesn't have much petrol," he lied.

"Well, OK. I'm parked on the street," she said, still clinging to his arm. "Your muscles are all tight," she said, squeezing his bicep through his jacket. "How come you're so tense?"

"You just excite me," he cracked, leading her quickly in the other direction, away from the car-park.

"Hey – what's the rush?" Lauren protested.

"I'm hungry," he lied. "Let's go and get a burger."

Did Shannon see me? he wondered. What is she doing there? Is she going to wait there all night?

He turned back to look.

"Oh!" He gaped in horror as he saw the flames shoot out from the front seat of his car.

Still standing a little in front of the car, Shannon stared at him, hands on her hips, just stood and stared, as still as a statue, bathed in the yellow glow of the fire.

Fourteen

"I have to tell you something, Shannon, and you have to listen to me," Jack said, softly, seriously.

She tugged at a strand of her hair, but didn't reply.

They were sitting on the sofa in her living room, its cushions worn and sagging. The only light came from a dim bulb in the back hallway.

She edged closer to him, her face covered in shadow. He could smell the sweet, flowery perfume she was wearing.

"Will you listen to me?" he asked softly. "I have the feeling that you do not listen to me, Shannon."

She leaned forward, bent her head, and brushed her hair against his cheek. It sent a shiver of excitement through him.

"Shannon . . . ?" He really wanted to talk to her, to communicate with her. He had to set things straight, once and for all.

106

She pressed her head against his shoulder, a tender gesture.

"Shannon . . . ?"

"You hurt me, Jack," she whispered.

He leaned away, tried to get some room between them. "That's what I want to talk to you about," he said.

The ceiling creaked. What was that sound? Footsteps? Was someone walking around upstairs?

"You hurt me," she repeated. She raised her head and stared at him, her dark eyes burning into his. "And when I get hurt, I hurt back," she told him, still whispering.

"That's what I wanted to talk to you about," he said, edging away, trying to back away from the warmth of her, the fragrance of her perfume. "You see, I can't see you. Ever again."

She stared at him, her face expressionless, beautiful in the dim light.

"I know we had something really special," Jack said. "But you have to understand that it's over. I really can't see you."

She remained silent. The only sounds now were the creaking of the ceiling, her soft, rhythmic breathing, the insistent pounding of his heart.

"Do you understand?" he asked, raising his voice for the first time.

"Let me see your hand," she said, reaching for him.

He pulled his arm away. "You broke my hand, Shannon. Why do you want to see it?"

"Let me see the other hand, baby. I want to tell your future."

"No," he insisted. "I'm *telling* you the future. I cannot see you again."

Her lips puckered into a childish pout.

"Do you understand? Do you finally understand?" Jack demanded.

"I'm very hurt," she said, still pouting. "You have hurt me a lot, Jack. And my brothers don't like it when I'm hurt."

As she said this, the floorboards creaked and groaned. The room filled with dark figures, moving quickly through the shadows, large figures, lumbering noisily.

A light went on overhead. Three enormous men stood in front of the sofa, glaring at Jack. Even though they were indoors, all three were wearing long trench coats with wide lapels. All three had round, red faces, topped with short-cropped white-blond hair.

"My brothers don't like people who hurt me, Jack," Shannon said in her whispery voice, speaking tonelessly, without any expression at all.

"Now, wait . . ." Jack started, suddenly terrified. He looked up at the three identical brothers looming menacingly over him, so big, so muscular, their faces locked on him, seething in silent anger.

"Get him," one of the brothers said, raising his arms as if to perform a stranglehold.

"Get him," the others grunted.

Jack uttered a low cry and shrank back on the sofa as the three enormous men circled it, then closed in on him.

Fifteen

The phone was ringing.

He stirred, pushed himself up, and squinting against the morning light, looked for Shannon's brothers.

The phone rang again.

"It was a dream," he said aloud, his throat still clogged with sleep.

Of *course* it was a dream. An ugly, frightening dream. But just a dream.

He picked up the phone and cleared his throat. "Hello?"

The dream lingered in his mind. He expected to hear Shannon at the other end.

"Hi, did I wake you?"

"Lauren?" He was relieved to hear her voice. He glanced at the clock. Ten-twenty.

"Who were you expecting?" she asked teasingly. "Your mystery girl?"

Her joke sent a shock wave down the back of his neck.

Did she know something? Did she mean something by that?

Of course not.

Don't go completely mental, Jack, he scolded himself.

"I guess I slept late," he said uncertainly. "What's going on?"

"That was so horrible with the car last night, I just wondered how you were," she said.

"I'm OK, I guess. Mum took it pretty well," he told her, remembering the night before with a shudder. It all came back to him in a series of ugly pictures flashing before his eyes: the flames licking up from the car, Shannon seeming to disappear into thin air along with her mysterious brother, Jack running to the car, the fire engines, the hoses, the crowd of onlookers.

"Did the firemen figure out what caused the fire?" Lauren asked.

"Yeah. They think it was a match," Jack told her. "They think someone came out from the game, lit up a cigarette, and tossed the match into my front seat. It was so rubbish of me to leave the window open."

Of course, Jack knew that wasn't how his car was set on fire. He knew that Shannon had done it. He could still see her standing there staring at him and Lauren as the flames grew higher and higher behind her.

I've got to talk to Shannon, he thought. I've got to make her see that this all has to stop.

He glanced down at his broken hand. It itched like crazy. He banged the cast against the wall, but it didn't help.

This all has to stop. It *has* to!

"Mum's making her famous waffles for breakfast," Lauren said.

"Is *that* what smells so good?" he joked, sniffing loudly into the receiver.

"Why don't you hurry up and get dressed and come over for breakfast?" Lauren suggested.

"Well, no I—"

"Don't say no," she interrupted. "Say yes."

"But I'm going to see you in a few hours at this stupid Junior Chamber of Commerce thing."

"Oh, I see," she replied sharply. "And seeing me twice in one day would be too much for you, huh?"

"OK. I'll be there in fifteen minutes," he quickly agreed. "Don't eat all the waffles before I get there."

"Me?!" she cried with exaggerated indignation. "You pig! I'm not the one who swallows the waffles whole! I wouldn't touch your stupid waffles!"

"Don't yell," he said softly.

"Why not?" she screamed.

"Because I have a broken hand."

She laughed. "You're weird, Singleton. Hurry over, OK? I want to show you the dress I'm wearing this afternoon. Wait till you see it. It's hilarious. It looks like something my grandmother would wear."

"Can't wait," he said sarcastically. He faked a loud yawn.

"Hey – be a good sport about this afternoon," she said.

"Huh?"

"Be a good boy at the Autumn Ball and maybe I'll buy you a balloon."

"See you," he said, and hung up.

When he came downstairs, his mother was on the phone with the insurance company about the car. "Be home in a few hours," he whispered. She looked up, concentrating on her conversation, and gave him a quick wave. "But I need a car right away. Can you get me a replacement?" she was saying.

Feeling guilty, Jack headed out the front door and began walking to Lauren's house, only four streets away. It was a clear, crisp day. The sky was bright blue and cloudless.

Much too nice a day to be cooped up with the Junior Chamber of Commerce, he thought unhappily.

The waffles cheered him up a little. Mrs DeMarco kept pouring more batter on the waffle iron, bringing replacements to the table so fast Jack could barely keep up. Finally, feeling stuffed, he begged her to stop. "I won't fit into my jacket this afternoon!" he told her.

"Speaking of that hideous jacket," said Lauren, getting up from the table, "come and see my dress." She grabbed his hand and dragged him to her room.

"Hey, what's wrong with my jacket?" he asked, pretending to be offended. They'd had this conversation before.

"It looks just like a horse blanket I saw at the riding stable last week," Lauren told him.

"Yeah, but what's *wrong* with it?" he joked.

They both laughed. She closed the door to her room, threw her arms around his neck, and kissed him. "You always make me happy," she said.

Normally he'd feel happy, too. But this morning, every nice thing Lauren said just made him feel guilty.

She pulled the dress out of the wardrobe. He agreed that it was weird-looking. It was a blue sheath dress made of some sort of shiny material. "I'm going to look like a grown-up," she said, holding it up in front of her. "And you're going to look like a horse!"

"Lay off my jacket," he grumbled, making a sour face.

She whinnied at him, doing a pretty good imitation of a horse.

"Give me a break, Lauren!" he cried.

She whinnied again, laughing. He started to chase her around the room. Laughing, they stumbled out onto the landing.

"It's still early," she said, taking his hand. "We don't have to be there till two. Come out into the garden for a while."

She led him downstairs and out through the sliding glass doors. They crossed the terrace, stopped to look at the covered swimming pool, then started walking slowly, arm in arm, down the wide, sloping lawn.

"Dad's really excited that you're going to intern at his place this summer," she said, taking a deep breath of the fresh, sweet-smelling air.

"Not as excited as I am," Jack told her.

"I think it's so cute how he's kind of adopted you," Lauren said chirpily. "I think he always wanted a son. Instead he got me."

"You're all right," Jack said, grinning.

"Thanks a bunch," she said sarcastically, giving him a playful shove.

She stopped suddenly. "What's that?"

Jack followed her stare. There was a small, dark object lying in the grass near the wooden fence.

"That's odd," Lauren said. "Let's see what it is."

As they stepped closer, walking quickly over the wet grass, the object came into view. It was a black cap, lying upside down.

"Hey – isn't that the Raiders cap you always wear?" Lauren asked.

Jack gasped.

"How did your cap get back here?" Lauren asked him, puzzled.

"I don't know," he said, overwhelmed by a sudden feeling of dread.

He held back while she ran to get the cap.

"Lauren? Wait!" he called.

But he was too late.

She bent over to pick up the cap, looked inside it, then, raising her hands to her face, started to scream.

Sixteen

"What is it?" Jack cried, running over to her, his heart pounding.

"It – it's Fluffernutter!" she wailed.

Jack put an arm around Lauren's heaving shoulders and stared into the cap. The white cat was dead, its blue eyes already sunken back in a gruesome, glassy stare. Its body had been bent and stuffed tightly into the baseball cap.

"Who did this?" Lauren wailed, tears pouring down her cheeks. "Who did this?"

Jack stood gaping at her. Lauren had always seemed to be in complete control. He had never seen her cry before.

"Fluffernutter!" she cried. She picked up the baseball cap and cradled it against her chest. "Poor Fluffernutter."

Shannon did this, Jack realized.

I left the cap at her house. She never returned it.

Until now.

She'll do *anything*, he thought. *Anything*. She doesn't care what she kills or who she hurts.

He stared at the cast on his hand. First Shannon took out her jealousy on me. And now she has taken it out on Lauren.

What am I going to do? What *can* I do?

I've go to stop Shannon. But how?

"Who did this?" Lauren demanded, staring at him now, still cradling the dead cat in her arms. "Who?"

"I don't know," Jack said softly, his arm around her tenderly. "I just can't imagine . . ."

How long can I keep lying to Lauren? he asked himself.

How many more horrors is Shannon going to commit before I'm forced to tell Lauren the truth?

"Who did this? Who did this?" Lauren repeated, holding the cat tightly, closing her eyes. Then she opened them and stared at Jack, her expression hardening. "How did Fluffernutter get in your cap? How did your cap get in my back garden?"

"I don't know," Jack lied. "I haven't seen the cap for days. I lost it over a week ago."

"You lost it?"

"Yeah. I've been looking and looking for it," he said. "I think maybe I must've left it at your house sometime."

"Poor Fluffernutter," Lauren said, wet tears covering her eyes again. "I just don't understand this." She stared hard at Jack, as if expecting him to have an answer.

118

He gently took the cap with its twisted corpse out of her hands and set it back down on the ground.

I've got to tell her the truth, he decided.

I've got to stop lying. I just can't take this any more.

I'll tell her about Shannon. Lauren will be hurt and upset, but she'll forgive me. And once she knows the truth, we can both go to the police. We can stop Shannon once and for all.

Jack took a deep breath. "Lauren – I have to tell you . . ."

But before he could say another word, a large, dark figure stepped up from behind and grabbed Jack by the shoulder.

Seventeen

Jack spun around in terror.

"Mr DeMarco!" he cried.

Lauren's father grinned at him, squeezing his shoulder. "Sorry if I startled you. How is my favourite couple today?" He was wearing a smartly tailored, black wool suit, already dressed for the afternoon affair.

"Dad – Fluffernutter is dead!" Lauren wailed, pointing down to the cap on the ground. "Somebody killed her!"

Mr DeMarco's broad smile shrank to an open-mouthed look of shock, and his normally ruddy face paled. He let go of Jack's shoulder as he saw the contents of the cap.

He didn't say anything. His mouth froze in an O of surprise and puzzlement. He leaned his head down to examine the cat, then looked up at Jack. "Isn't that your cap?"

Jack felt his face grow red. "Yes," he muttered. "It's been lost for days."

"How strange," Mr DeMarco said, tucking his tie back under his suit jacket with a trembling hand. "How strange."

It isn't strange at all, Jack thought guiltily.

I could explain it to you in less than a minute.

But the desire to explain, to tell the truth, had left him. He knew he couldn't face both Lauren and Mr DeMarco together. They would be so disappointed in him. So hurt by his betrayal.

Things would never be the same again, Jack realized.

Silently, he walked back to the house with them. The walk took only a few minutes, but it seemed like an eternity.

The Junior Chamber of Commerce Autumn Ball was held in the ballroom of the Sheraton hotel. The room was vast, with rows of crystal chandeliers suspended from the high ceilings over the dozens of round banquetting tables spread over the room. There were tall flower arrangements as a centrepiece on every table. A large parquet dance floor stood to the right of the tables. In the front of the room, beyond the table of honour, stood a low stage where the dinner-jacketed orchestra sat.

Jack immediately saw that he and Lauren were just about the only young people in the room. They arrived a little after two to find the place already crowded, the orchestra already playing some lilting lift music, waiters passing through the room with silver trays of hors d'oeuvres, a long line at the punch bowl.

Jack's mother had her platinum hair piled high on her head and moussed until it stood as stiff as a sculpture. She wore her new cocktail dress, the brightest dress in the room. But Jack didn't mind. He was used to his mother's flamboyant style. Actually, he realized, the clothes she wore and her platinum hair were the only flamboyant things about her.

Mr and Mrs DeMarco were somewhat sombrely dressed, especially in comparison with Mrs Singleton. Mr DeMarco wore his black wool suit with a dark, narrow tie. Mrs DeMarco had chosen a tailored grey suit, the colour just a shade darker than her greying hair, with a high-collared white shirt, offset by a dark blue silk scarf worn loosely as a tie around her neck.

Lauren actually looked sensational in the blue sheath dress she had made fun of that morning. It had seemed dowdy and old-fashioned when she held it up in her room. But on her, Jack thought, it became a very sexy party dress.

But of course, none of them were in a party mood this afternoon.

Mr DeMarco had buried Fluffernutter by the fence in the back garden. Jack's Raiders cap had been thrown into the rubbish bin.

They had all come to the hotel together in Mr DeMarco's BMW. Mr DeMarco had tried to cheer everyone up by telling funny stories he had heard at work. But, still thinking about the murdered cat in the back garden, they were a pretty grim crowd.

Now they entered the ballroom with forced smiles. The adults hurried to greet friends, shaking hands, kissing cheeks. Jack and Lauren got in line for some punch, both of them feeling tense and uncomfortable.

Jack had dreaded this afternoon for weeks. He knew it would be boring and difficult, keeping a smile plastered to his face for hours as people, mostly friends of the DeMarcos, congratulated Lauren and him, slapped him on the back, and told them what a good-looking couple they made and how proud everyone was of them.

But after what had happened, it was even harder than Jack had imagined to keep it together. He didn't feel like smiling at these people, like making small talk about the warm winter they'd had so far, about school, and about the Tigers and what a shame it was that Jack had broken his hand and couldn't finish the season.

Knowing how his hand had been broken, knowing how Lauren's poor cat had been killed – knowing that he himself was largely responsible for the terrible things that were happening – was driving Jack over the edge.

He felt like tearing off his stupid sports jacket and the tie that was choking him and tossing them in the bin. Then he'd run out the door and keep running.

Away from Lauren. Away from the DeMarcos, even though they'd been so nice, so giving. Away from his mother. Away from Glenview. Away from everyone he knew.

Away from . . . Shannon.

He'd run and run and never stop.

"What are you thinking about?" Lauren asked, filling a glass with dark purple punch and handing it to him, some of the liquid spilling over the sides.

"I'm thinking about how great you look in that dress," he lied. He spilled a little of the punch back into the gigantic crystal punch bowl.

She forced a smile. "And I'm thinking how that jacket *still* looks like a horse blanket!"

He laughed, pleased to see her smile again. They headed towards a corner, away from the dance floor crowded with people talking and laughing, where they could drink the awful, sweet punch in peace.

But there was no escape today.

"Kids! Kids!" cried an excited woman's voice, and Mrs Benedict, the president of the Junior Chamber of Commerce and organizer of this event, came hurrying over. She was a tall woman, as thin as a rake, dressed in a straight, black skirt that emphasized her slimness. She wore four or five huge, sparkling rings on her fingers and had at least six strands of gold and emerald beads around her neck, which clattered noisily as she came running up to them.

"Oh, we're all so excited!" she gushed, beaming at them both. "You two look wonderful."

Lauren thanked her. Jack nodded, nervously straightening his light brown hair with one hand.

"We're going to have lunch. Then I'm going to present your awards to you," Mrs Benedict said. "And the cheque, of course," she added, and laughed a high-pitched laugh.

"Thank you," Lauren said. Jack repeated her words, shifting his weight uncomfortably, staring down at his empty punch cup.

"We're all so proud of you," Mrs Benedict said. "You're both just so exceptional. And I understand you're both going to Princeton next autumn. How wonderful!" She stopped. And blinked. "I'm embarrassing you, aren't I," she said in a subdued voice.

"No, not at all," Lauren said quickly.

"Everyone's being so nice to us," Jack added.

"I didn't mean to make you uncomfortable," Mrs Benedict said. "I know this must be hard for you. My son Oliver – you know Oliver – well, he refused to come today.

He's at home playing video games. I'm sure you'd rather be doing that, too. It's just so refreshing to meet two truly *nice* young people these days."

"Thanks," Lauren and Jack said. They both shook hands with Mrs Benedict, and she walked away, her necklaces clinking.

"She's not so bad," Lauren said, watching her stop to greet some late arrivals.

"Her son's a total nerd," Jack said, sniggering.

"I don't think anyone wearing that sports jacket should call anyone else a total nerd," Lauren cracked. "And what about that tie? Is that a clip-on?"

Jack made an unhappy face, but he was secretly pleased that Lauren was making jokes again. "Save my place against the wall here, OK?" he asked, handing her his empty punch glass.

"Where are you going? Are you ducking out?" she asked suspiciously.

"No," he told her. "I'm going to the gents. We can't be together *every* second, you know."

She stuck her tongue out at him. He rolled his eyes and started off across the room.

"Hey – what happened to your hand?" a middle-aged man in a red blazer asked as Jack passed.

"Hunting accident," Jack replied. He didn't know why he

said that. The words just came to him. He decided he was starting to feel a little better, too.

He was making his way past the rows of tables when a guy he recognized as a cousin of the DeMarcos came hurrying up to him, a concerned look on his face. "Hey, Jack!" he called.

Jack tried to remember his name. "You're Paul, right?"

"Right," the guy said, not smiling. "I think you should go to the lobby."

"Huh?" Jack wasn't sure he heard him correctly.

"I think you're needed in the lobby," Paul repeated, his forehead wrinkled with concern. "There's someone out there. A girl."

Jack had a heavy, sinking feeling. "A girl? In the lobby? Why do they need me?"

"Well . . ." Paul reached a hand over his shoulder and rubbed the back of his neck. "Sorry. Stiff neck. I woke up with it."

"What about this girl?" Jack demanded.

"She doesn't have an invitation, so they're not letting her in. But she says she's your date." Paul looked meaningfully across the room at Lauren, who was still talking to her father.

"My date? That's complete rubbish," Jack said. "They should just send her away. I don't know who it could be." He lowered his voice confidentially to Paul. "Why would anyone want to crash *this* party?" He laughed.

Paul didn't seem to catch his humour. "Well, the lunch is going to be really something," he replied, studying Jack's face. "You'd better hurry up. The hotel people are waiting for you, Jack."

"OK," Jack said, realizing he had no choice. He could feel all of his muscles tense as he turned and walked to the ballroom doorway. He could hear his mother calling him from somewhere near the stage, but he just kept walking, taking long, steady strides.

What am I going to do? he thought, trying to fight down the panic he felt.

What am I going to say to Shannon? How can I get rid of her before anyone sees her?

A gong rang behind him in the ballroom. He heard chairs being scraped across the floor. Lunch was being served. He had felt hungry a few moments before, but now his stomach was tied in a knot.

He stepped out into the hallway. Two uniformed hotel workers, serious-looking young men with slicked-back black hair and hard expressions, were standing beside a wooden desk that had been set up to check off guests on the list as they arrived.

And there was Shannon. Standing between them, her arms crossed over her chest.

Jack stopped at the doorway and stared at her.

What did she think she was doing? How did she have the nerve to come here?

Her hair had been carefully brushed for once, he saw, and tied back with a red hair ribbon. She was wearing a bright red dress, very tight, cut low in the front, very short, ending only halfway down her thighs.

She unfolded her arms to gesture at the two hotel guards, and Jack saw that she was wearing short, red gloves that matched her dress.

Is that her idea of dressing up? Jack thought. He was no fashion expert, but he knew that Shannon didn't look right for *this* place!

She looked so . . . tacky. Why had he ever thought she was cute? What had he seen in her?

He cleared his throat nervously and started towards her.

She saw him while he was still halfway across the lobby and called to him. "Jack – here I am!"

"Shannon – what are you doing here?" he asked coldly, stepping up to the desk. One of the guards kept Shannon back, holding her by the arm.

"Tell them who I am, baby. They don't believe me," she said in her little-girl voice, making her eyes really big.

"She doesn't have an invitation, sir," the guard said, letting go of Shannon's arm. "Is she with you?"

"I'm your date, right, Jack?" Shannon asked before Jack could reply to the guard.

Jack stared at her. "Shannon, I can't believe you're doing this," he said, his heart pounding but his voice low and steady.

"Tell them, Jack," she said, smiling at him, ignoring his words. Her lips were covered with bright red lipstick. Some of it had smeared onto her front teeth.

"Why, Shannon?" Jack asked, more of a plea than a question. "Why are you here?" He glanced back to the ballroom entrance, hoping no one was coming to look for him.

"I'm your date, baby," she insisted in her tiniest voice. "Tell them." Her voice remained tiny, but her eyes narrowed and her expression grew hard.

She pulled away from the guards and latched her arm around his.

"Sir, is she with you or not?" the guard asked impatiently.

"Tell them, baby," she said, pulling him towards the ballroom doors, her face hard, determined. "I'm your date. I'm coming in. I want to meet everybody."

Eighteen

"No," Jack cried, trying to disentangle himself from her. "You can't!"

"I'm going in with you, Jack." She clung to his arm, holding him tightly, staring up at him, her dark-lipsticked mouth set in a stubborn pout.

My life will be ruined, he thought, feeling himself overcome with panic. If I walk into the ballroom with her, if Lauren sees me with her, if everyone sees her – my life will be ruined.

That's what Shannon wants. She wants to ruin my life.

"No!" he cried again, and pulled himself free of her grasp.

"Miss . . ." one of the hotel guards called, stepping around the desk, an alarmed look on his face.

"Stop, miss," the other one called, looking suspiciously at Jack.

"I'm your date. I'm going in there!" Shannon screamed. Her dark eyes flared angrily. Then she spun away from him and started to run across the lobby towards the ballroom, moving awkwardly in her red high-heeled shoes.

"Stop her!" Jack pleaded.

She's going to humiliate me, he thought. She's going to humiliate me in front of everyone I care about.

He hesitated only a second. Then, seeing that the two guards were frozen in indecision, he took off after her.

She turned her head back as she ran and saw him coming. "I'm going in!" she yelled.

"No!" He leaped after her, and, ignoring the cast on his hand, made a diving tackle.

"Let go!" she shrieked.

His arm circled her waist. The force of his dive sent them both sprawling to the lobby carpet.

"Aaaiii!" he screamed in pain as she landed on his cast.

Heads turned. A woman across the lobby gasped. The two guards were moving fast towards Jack.

"Let go! Let go! Let go!" Ignoring the pain shooting up his arm, he pulled himself up and forced her down onto her back. She swung her fists up at him. But he had her securely pinned on the floor.

Crying out, she reached up and pulled his tie hard, choking him. As he struggled to loosen the tie with one good hand, she pulled herself out from under him, shoved him hard, and rolled on top of him.

This can't be happening, Jack thought, looking up to see a horrified crowd around them. The two guards were bent over them, trying to pull Shannon off him.

"I'm going in!" she shouted, as the guard lifted her up by the arms. "I'm going in!" Her hair had come loose from the ribbon and was flying wildly about her face.

"What's going on here?" an important-looking man in a dark blue suit cried, breaking through the circle of onlookers.

"I'm going in," Shannon insisted, as the two guards struggled to pull her to the front exit.

Somewhat dazed, Jack climbed to his feet. He touched his cheek. It felt wet. Looking at his hand, he realized his face was bleeding. Shannon must have scratched him as they scuffled.

Trying to catch his breath, he glanced towards the ballroom. Luckily no one had come out to witness the embarrassing scene. He looked around the crowd in the lobby and didn't recognize anyone.

"Are you OK?" the man in the dark suit asked.

"Yeah. I think so," Jack said, holding his cheek. The hand under the cast throbbed with pain.

Shannon was being pulled, struggling and screaming, out of the lobby. People gasped and moved quickly out of the way as the two guards, one on each side, tried to remove her.

I've got to get back inside, Jack thought, feeling a little relieved. Lauren must be wondering where I am.

First, I've got to find a gents and wash off this blood.

Then he gasped as he saw Shannon kick one of the guards hard in the knee. The guard cried out in pain and dropped to the floor.

With a burst of speed, Shannon broke away from the other startled guard, and came running back towards Jack, heading for the ballroom.

"I'm your date, Jack!" she yelled, staring at him, her eyes wild and frantic as she passed him, running awkwardly in the heels. "I'm your date! You can't keep me out!"

"Shannon – stop!" he yelled. He grabbed her again with his one good hand, and held on tight.

"Young man, I – I cannot allow this," the man in the blue suit sputtered. "You and your girlfriend must leave at once."

"But I'm going in," Shannon insisted.

"Shannon – please," Jack begged, holding on desperately to her arm.

Suddenly, she stopped struggling. She looked up at him with her little-girl face and brushed his bleeding cheek tenderly with her gloved hand. "Tell them I'm your date, Jack."

"Young man, I must insist . . ." the important-looking man, obviously the hotel manager, said.

An idea flashed into Jack's mind, an idea born of panic, of desperation.

"Shannon – if I take you out next weekend, will you go home now?" he asked, not loosening his grip on her arm.

"You're hurting me," she cried, staring into his eyes.

Reluctantly he let go of her arm. "How about it, Shannon? Please? I'll take you out on Saturday night. I promise."

"Really?" she asked in her tiny voice. "Just you and me?"

"Yes. Just you and me," he said quickly, seeing that she was considering it. "You go home now, and I promise I'll take you out next weekend."

"You promise?"

"I promise."

"Hope to die?" she asked.

Something about the way she said that gave him a chill. "I promise," he repeated, still breathing heavily, his chest heaving, his heart pounding. "Please, Shannon. Go home, OK? And Saturday night will be our night."

She stared up at him for a long moment, pulling loose strands of hair away from her face, "OK," she said finally.

He breathed a loud sigh of relief, then bent down and picked up her red hair ribbon from the floor. "Good," he said softly, handing it to her.

He looked back towards the ballroom. No one had come

out. He could hear voices and the clink of dishes and glasses. They must be halfway through lunch, he thought.

"Walk me to the door?" Shannon asked, pulling the red ribbon back and forth through her hand.

"OK," Jack quickly agreed.

Anything to get her out of here!

What am I going to tell Lauren?

He felt his cheek. The bleeding seemed to have slowed. Some dark, dried blood flaked off on his fingers.

"I didn't mean to hurt you, baby," Shannon said softly.

"It's OK," he replied, leading her quickly to the door. People were staring at them from all over the huge lobby.

"You'll come to my house on Saturday night?"

He pushed open the glass door and guided her out of the building. "Promise," he said.

The sky was overcast with dark clouds hovering low. It looked as if it might snow. The sudden cold made the cut on his face sting.

She looked up at him one more time as if trying to read in his face whether or not he was telling the truth. Then, without saying another word, she turned and began running along the path that led past the hotel car-park, her clunky red shoes clicking over the pavement.

What have I done? he thought. And then: What am I going to do?

He watched her as she passed the car-park, running so awkwardly, not looking back. And then he saw the figure step out from behind a parked car in the main drive.

It was Shannon's brother. Jack recognized him immediately even though he had never clearly seen his face. He recognized him from his enormous size and from his long coat.

The man was moving quickly towards Jack, pointing at him, calling to him even though he was too far away for Jack to make out the words.

Does her brother follow her everywhere? Jack wondered. What does he want?

Jack had no intention of waiting to find out. He spun around, pulled open the door, and nearly knocking over an elderly couple who were trying to exit, bounded back into the hotel.

He won't follow me into the ballroom, Jack decided. Taking long, quick strides, he headed across the lobby and down the hall towards the ballroom at the back.

He was nearly there when he remembered that his face was cut. Looking down, he saw that his shirt had come untucked during his wrestling match with Shannon, the white flaps hanging down over his trousers. A button had been torn off his sports jacket. His tie hung loose and crooked.

What should he do now?

Behind him, he saw Shannon's brother lumber into the lobby, looking in all directions, obviously searching for Jack.

The ballroom offered safety. But Jack knew he couldn't go back in there looking the way he did. He had to get himself cleaned up a bit first.

Praying that the hulking figure hadn't spotted him, Jack ducked into the gents, pulling the door closed behind him. He looked for a door lock, but there was none.

Moving to the mirrors over the row of sinks, he examined himself. The cut wasn't as bad as he had feared. It was just a scratch, actually. He picked up some paper towels from beside the sink, wet them, and dabbed the dried blood away.

Unfortunately, he had bled onto his shirt collar. He tried dabbing at the stain with the wet paper towel, but it only smeared the blood, making a larger stain.

He combed his hair, surprised that his hands were still trembling. Then he tucked in his shirt and retied his tie.

I don't look too bad, he thought.

Maybe I can go back in and pretend nothing happened.

And then, in the mirror, he saw the door open and Shannon's brother step in.

Nineteen

Gaping into the mirror, Jack hesitated for only a second. As the big man moved through the narrow corridor that led to the sinks, Jack darted to the cubicles. He leaped into the nearest one and pulled the cubicle door closed, latching it silently.

Did he see me?

Does he know I'm in here?

His heart pounding, Jack climbed up onto the toilet, hunched on the seat, keeping his feet off the floor so they couldn't be seen in the space beneath the cubicle door.

His chest felt tight. He had a strong urge to cough. His fright was making it hard to breathe.

Hunched on top of the toilet seat, he held his breath, forced himself not to cough . . . and listened.

The heavy footsteps against the marble floor grew louder. Closer.

Peering down beneath the cubicle door, Jack could see the man's shadow on the floor. He was standing right in front of the cubicle.

He knows I'm here, Jack thought, still holding his breath even though it felt as if his lungs were about to burst. He knows.

He's standing there, waiting for me.

He's not going to make a move until I come out.

The shadow on the white tile floor shifted. Jack could hear the man's shoes scrape as he moved.

Is he coming to get me? Jack wondered, frozen in fear.

Is he going to force open the door, grab me, and pull me out?

The shadow on the floor seemed to freeze in place. Then, as Jack stared down from his uncomfortable perch, it slid out of sight.

The shoes scraped heavily, moving away.

Jack still didn't breathe, listening to the shoes move against the tiles. When he heard the gents door squeak open and then close, he exhaled loudly, but still didn't move.

He listened carefully.

Silence.

Struggling to catch his breath, he climbed down off the toilet seat. He unlocked the door, pulled it open, and stepped out.

Shannon's brother was waiting for him at the first sink. "Tricked you," he said, smiling. He had short blond hair, a round, red face with small grey eyes over a pug nose.

He took a step towards Jack and pointed with two fingers. "I want to talk to you." He had a reedy, high-pitched voice, a voice much too small for a man his size.

"I've got to g-go," Jack managed to stammer. With a determined burst of speed, he ran towards Shannon's brother, then dodged away from him and raced through the narrow corridor to the exit.

"Wait . . ." the brother cried, lurching towards Jack.

But Jack already had the gents' door open. He ran through it and across the lobby, past the two uniformed guards at the desk outside the ballroom door and into the ballroom.

Dessert was being served from trolleys. Coffee was being poured from silver coffeepots. The room was quiet except for a few low murmurs.

Why isn't anyone talking? Jack wondered, his eyes surveying the room. He quickly understood why. Mrs Benedict was standing in the centre of the main table, about to speak.

Forcing a smile to his face, hoping he looked at least a little normal, Jack made his way through the tables to the front, being careful not to look at anyone. He didn't stop

141

until he reached his table. Then he found his seat and slid in silently beside Lauren.

She turned immediately and stared at him questioningly. "Jack, where've you been?" she whispered. "You missed lunch."

"We're so proud of both of them," Mrs Benedict was saying into the microphone, standing just a few feet away, holding a stack of notecards in front of her. "Before I call them up to award them their prizes, let me tell you a little about these two young people and their accomplishments."

Lauren continued to stare at him, searching his face. Suddenly, her eyes widened in surprise. "Jack – you've been bleeding. What did you do to your face?" she whispered.

"I tripped," he whispered. "In the gents. I fell onto the sink."

Her expression remained one of bewilderment. He wasn't sure whether she believed him or not.

"As you can see, both of them are citizens of the community as well as students," Mrs Benedict was saying. She looked over at Jack and Lauren and blinked hard when she saw that they weren't paying attention to her speech.

"You're sweating like a pig," Lauren whispered loudly. "Jack, are you OK?"

I'll *never* be OK, Jack thought.

Never.

Not as long as Shannon is around.

She's never going to leave me alone. She's never going to quit.

All my plans, all my hopes – my whole life – it's all ruined.

"I'm going to to call Jack and Lauren up now, so let's give them a warm round of applause," Mrs Benedict said.

Twenty

Jack called Lauren on Wednesday night. He had carefully rehearsed what he was going to say, but he was very nervous, uncertain of how she would react.

The phone rang once, and he dropped the receiver. Doing everything with one hand was really difficult, he had discovered. The big cast had been removed on Tuesday, replaced by one that was smaller but just as clunky.

He fumbled around on the floor of his room for the receiver. When he managed to return it to his ear, Lauren was already on the other end. "Hello? Hello?"

"Hi, it's me," he said.

"Jack, have you been avoiding me?" she asked.

"Huh? What are you talking about?"

Did she suspect something about Shannon?

"I haven't seen you since Saturday afternoon," Lauren said.

"Yeah. I know," he said. "I've been working and stuff."

"You've been kind of weird lately," she said. "I mean, weirder than usual."

"Is that a compliment?" he joked.

"Is anything the matter?" she asked.

What a question!

"No," he said. "Not really." There was an awkward silence, and then he began his prepared speech. "Lauren, would it be OK if we don't go out on Saturday night?"

"What?" The question seemed to take her by surprise.

"You see, my cousin is sick up in Meritville, and I thought I'd drive up and see him on Saturday night."

"I thought you didn't have a car," she said suspiciously.

"Mum got a hire car from the insurance company. It's actually much better than our car," he said.

"But can you drive with one hand?" she asked.

She suspects something, he thought. That's why she's asking so many questions.

"Yeah. No problem," he said. "I know we usually go out on Saturdays, but Eddie has always been a real pal and—"

"Jack, I think you're confused," she said, suddenly sounding very cross.

"What?"

This wasn't going right, he realized. She was supposed to be sympathetic. She was supposed to tell him it was perfectly all right for him to go and visit his sick cousin.

"How could you forget your own birthday?" she cried.

"Huh?"

"You can't visit your cousin on Saturday night, Jack. That's the night we're celebrating your birthday, remember? I've made big plans. I'm picking you up at your house at nine and taking you somewhere very special." She paused and then added sharply, "Doesn't *any* of this ring a bell?"

"Oh. Yeah," he said.

How could he have forgotten his own birthday? Lauren had made such a fuss about how she was going to plan something really cool.

Oh, well, he thought, sighing. Lauren isn't picking me up till nine. That'll give me time to get over to Shannon's early. I'll talk to Shannon, tell her I can't ever see her again, get everything straight with her once and for all, and be back at my house by nine.

"I feel like a total dork," he told Lauren. "I – I just wasn't thinking clearly. Forget everything I said. I'll go and visit my cousin on Sunday."

"That's better," she said. But she still sounded very suspicious.

"Uh . . . Lauren?"

He had this sudden urge to tell her how sorry he was. He wanted to tell her that he hadn't meant to mess everything up. He wanted to tell her that Shannon didn't mean anything to him, that he didn't even like Shannon, that she was a mistake, a horrible mistake that he had regretted from the first night he had met her.

He felt like telling Lauren everything, just letting it all spill out. Not to cleanse himself. Not to make himself feel better. But just to let Lauren know that he didn't like having to lie to her, that he didn't like what Shannon had forced him to become.

"Yes?" Lauren asked, a little impatiently.

"I just want you to know I care about you," he said. His throat tightened. He couldn't say any more.

"Me, too," she said quickly.

"No matter what happens," he added.

"What?" she cried. "What do you mean? Jack?"

"I'll call you," he said and gently hung up the phone.

Twenty-One

Saturday was grey and cold. A sharp wind blew down from the north, toppling rubbish bins, sweeping the fallen dead leaves over the front garden like a crackling, brown river. The sun never appeared, and by late afternoon it was as dark as midnight.

Jack didn't notice the wind or the cold as he climbed into the white hire car a little after six o'clock to drive to Shannon's house. Thinking about her, about all she had done, about all she *could* do to ruin his life, he had felt edgy all day. But now, as he backed down the drive and headed towards the Old Village, his nervousness gave way to anger.

He had had only one date with Shannon. He had made no promises to her. He hadn't misled her in any way. What right did she have to keep pestering him, to follow him, to call him constantly, to try to invade his life?

She had no right. No right at all.

His mind whirled as he repeated over and over the things he planned to say to her. All of his attempts to get through to her, to make her stop, to get rid of her, had failed.

But not tonight, he told himself. Not tonight.

Tonight would be different. Tonight he would *make* her understand. Tonight he would make her *promise* to leave him alone.

And if she didn't agree?

He would talk to her parents. Or her brothers. He would tell them how unbalanced Shannon was. How dangerous.

Dangerous.

Well, Jack thought, I can be dangerous, too.

I can get tough if I have to.

Distracted by his angry thoughts, he sped through a stop sign. The squeal of another car's brakes alerted him to what he had done, but he didn't look back.

I'm going to make this short, he told himself, glancing down at the digital clock on the dashboard. Six-twenty.

He knew he had to be back home by nine, when Lauren planned to pick him up.

No problem, he thought.

As he drove into Shannon's neighbourhood, the houses passing by in the darkness were smaller and closer together. A burst of wind shook the car. He gripped the wheel tighter with his left hand, his other hand resting uselessly on his lap.

Halfway down the street, he squealed to a stop. He had driven right past Shannon's house. Cursing to himself, he threw the car into reverse and backed up along the curb. He parked at the bottom of her dirt driveway. Then he turned off the engine and climbed out, slamming the door behind him.

The house was dark except for a dim yellow light glowing behind the lowered blind in the front window. Jack jogged up the drive, ducking his head against the strong wind.

Why did I ever come here? he thought.

Why did I ever get involved with her?

He couldn't decide if he was more angry at Shannon or at himself. His temples throbbed as he climbed the two steps of her front porch. He felt strange, out of control, angry, and nervous – and a little frightened.

Taking a deep breath, he raised his hand to knock on the front door, and it was pulled open.

Shannon stood in the pale yellow light. She was dressed all in white, in a short, straight skirt and a white cotton jumper. Her red hair shone in the light, falling softly down in front of her shoulders.

She smiled at him, her dark eyes lighting up.

She looks like a little angel, Jack thought.

What a joke.

"Hi, baby. You're late," she said softly.

Stepping into the small front room, he didn't return her smile. "Hi," he said, keeping his expression hard.

"Let me hang up your coat," she said, reaching up to help pull off his jacket.

"No. I'm not staying long," he said sharply, looking around at the threadbare furniture, the peeling wallpaper, the bare floorboards. "Are your parents at home? Or your brothers?"

She gave him a devilish look. "No, baby. Don't worry. No one's at home. We're all alone." She took his jacket and hung it up.

She smelled sweet and flowery. He realized she was wearing a lot of perfume.

"Please don't call me baby," he said sharply.

When she turned around, she had a slightly mocking expression on her face. "Why not, baby?" she asked in her whispery voice.

"Because I'm *not* your baby!" he shouted.

She put her hand gently on his shoulder. "I made you a special dinner. Because this is such a special night."

He stared at her, surprised. "You cooked dinner?"

"Yes. Just for the two of us. Look." She pointed to a small table in the adjoining room. It had been set for two. A single candle glimmered in the centre. "Surprised?"

"Shannon, I'm sorry. I'm not going to stay," Jack said. He struggled to remember what he had planned to say, what he had rehearsed over and over in his mind all week. But he was drawing a blank.

"Come and sit down, Jack," she said, taking his hand.

He pulled his hand away. "Didn't you hear me?"

"How's your hand?" she asked, studying the cast. "It doesn't hurt any more, does it?"

"Shannon – don't ignore me," he said, feeling his anger rise.

"That was such a shame, such a nasty accident," she said, pushing her lipsticked mouth into a pout.

"It wasn't an accident," he said, glaring at her. "You did it deliberately."

"I wouldn't hurt you. You're my baby," she said softly. She reached up and grabbed the back of his head with both hands. Then she pulled his head down and pressed her lips against his.

She smelled so sweet. Her lips were so soft.

"*No!*" he screamed.

It was hard to pull away from her, especially with just one useful hand. She grasped the back of his head, holding him tightly. It was no longer a tender hold. It was violent, desperate.

Finally he managed to duck out of her grasp. He backed

away, holding his hand up as if it were a shield. "Stop it, Shannon."

"But what's the matter? Don't you *like* me any more?" Her voice sounded tiny and hurt.

"No," he said flatly.

She stared into his eyes. "You're not being nice to me, Jack."

"I came here to say leave me alone," he said, staring right back at her. "Leave me alone, Shannon. Don't call me. Don't follow me. Don't come to see me."

"I made such a nice dinner for us," she said.

"I want you to leave me alone. And I want you to leave my friends alone," he continued.

"I want this night to be special," she said softly.

"Aren't you listening to me?" he screamed. He could feel himself losing it, but he didn't care.

He had to make her hear him.

He *had* to!

"Listen to me, Shannon. I'm leaving now. Right now. And I'm never coming back. Do you hear me?"

"Don't leave," she said, her face expressionless now. Her smile had faded; her eyes lost their sparkle. "I don't think you should leave."

"What are you going to do? Break my *other* hand?" he cried.

"No," she said softly, "if you leave, I'll do something worse."

"Worse?" His chest was heaving. He had never felt such anger, such frustration.

"I'll tell Lauren," she said.

She waited for him to react, but he just glared at her.

"I'll tell Lauren everything," Shannon said, her face a pale, cold mask, revealing no emotion at all. "I'll go and see her. I'll tell her that you want to be with *me* now."

"No, you won't!" he screamed. "You won't!"

In a total rage, he grabbed her narrow shoulders and began to shake her.

The next few seconds became a noisy blur.

He suddenly felt as if he weren't here in this shabby, dimly-lit living room, as if he were somewhere above it, hovering over the room, watching the boy and girl struggle beneath him.

It wasn't him shaking Shannon so violently. It wasn't him roaring out his rage and frustration. It wasn't him making her head snap back like that, her long hair tossing wildly over her face, then behind her shoulders.

He wasn't doing it. He wasn't struggling with her, pushing her, choking her, slamming her small body against the dark wall.

"You've ruined my life! You've ruined my life!"

He wasn't crying out like that. He wasn't making her cry out.

He was above it, outside it, away from them, watching them.

And then suddenly the blur, the violent blur cleared.

And he saw everything so clearly.

Shannon was on the floor, crumpled in such a strange position, her head tilted at such a strange angle, her white skirt up over her pale thighs.

Her eyes were closed.

He could see everything so clearly.

Her eyes were closed, and she wasn't breathing.

So clear. So clear.

He had killed her.

Twenty-Two

I didn't kill Shannon, he thought, staring down at her, his eyes focusing and unfocusing.

I didn't kill her.

I'm the quarterback. I was player of the year last season.

I should've been player of the year again *this* season.

I'm too young.

I hardly knew her.

So how could I have killed her?

Lauren and I are the perfect couple. Everyone is so happy for us.

So happy.

I couldn't kill Shannon.

I've already been accepted at Princeton. Of course, I haven't heard from the scholarship people yet. But it's almost a sure thing.

Lauren and I will be there together.

It seems we've always been together.

We belong together. We're the perfect couple.

So I couldn't have killed Shannon.

"Get up, Shannon!" he yelled. He nudged her side with the toe of his trainer.

"Get up! Get up – please!"

He stood over her unmoving form. He couldn't bend down. He wanted to, but he couldn't move. He could only stand there.

Maybe I'm dead, too, he thought.

No. That's crazy. Crazy.

I'm the quarterback, Jack Singleton.

I'm the perfect couple.

There's a place waiting for me at Mr DeMarco's agency.

So I can't be dead. And neither can Shannon.

He could see everything so clearly, every detail in the room, every thread in Shannon's white cotton jumper, every hair on her head. Her hair was splayed out on the floor. Her legs were bent beneath her.

Lauren and I are the couple of the year, he thought.

He tried to remember his little brother's name. Why couldn't he think of it?

I'm not thinking clearly, he realized, staring down at her hair, so tangled and wild.

I can see very clearly. But I'm not thinking clearly.

He turned and walked over to the worn sofa. He dropped down onto it, closed his eyes, and rubbed his eyelids with the fingers of his good hand.

Charlie. That's his name.

OK. That's a little better.

He sat with his eyes closed for a long time, waiting for the panic to subside.

I'm just not thinking clearly. I've got to think clearly.

What do I do now?

She can't be dead. So what do I do now?

After all, I'm the quarterback.

Coach Hawkins is really going to yell at me about this.

I'm still not thinking clearly.

Charlie. His name is Charlie.

That's good. That's good for a start. But what do I *do* now?

He got up and walked back to her. "Aren't you going to move?" he asked softly. "Isn't dinner going to get cold?"

Aren't *you* going to get cold?

He had to do something to clear his head. He would never think clearly if he stood staring down at her, waiting for her to move.

He would never get his scholarship.

He would never pass Go and collect two hundred.

I've got to get out of here, he realized.

I've got to go somewhere and think. I'm not thinking clearly here. If I go away, I'll be able to figure everything out.

And then I'll go to Princeton. With Lauren.

I'll call Lauren right now. We can go to Princeton tonight.

No. He wasn't thinking clearly. Lauren wasn't at home.

She wasn't at home.

An idea flashed into his spinning head. Even in the confusion, he knew he could work out what to do if he got out of that house. He knew the cold air would help clear his head. Getting away from her body would help drive away his panic.

Her body?

Why did he think of her as a body now? She couldn't be dead.

He was too young.

And he was very smart. All the tests showed it.

He moved quickly to the front door, grabbed his jacket, and struggled into it, pulling it over his broken hand first, then easing his good hand through the other sleeve.

I'm not thinking clearly. I'm just not thinking clearly.

He searched the jacket pocket until he found the car keys. Then he pulled open the front door and started out.

A strong gust of wind blew him back.

I'm not thinking clearly. I've got to get away, go somewhere quiet, somewhere peaceful to think.

But I can't leave Shannon here.

She's not dead. But what if her parents come home? What if they find her lying on the floor, all twisted like that? They might *think* she's dead.

And I could get into trouble. Bad trouble.

Or what if her brothers come home? They could make a mistake, too. They could think she's dead. And then they'd come after me. Like that one huge brother of hers.

I'm not thinking clearly.

I'd better take her with me. Yes. I'll take her with me. And when I'm feeling a little better, a little calmer, a little quieter, I'll know what to do.

Picking Shannon up was hard, especially with only one good hand. Slinging her over his shoulder was even harder.

Luckily she was small and light.

Not as light as a feather, he thought. But light enough to carry out to the car.

She still felt warm as he draped her over his shoulder, holding her around the back of her legs with one arm. He made his way unsteadily to the front door, thought about getting her a coat, but decided he couldn't put her down again.

Out into the blustery wind. The front garden was dark. There was no porch light. The neighbours couldn't see him.

She started to get heavier as he carried her down the dirt drive. She was slipping off his shoulder.

Just a few more feet, he thought. The wind seemed to be blowing at him from all directions at once, making it hard to move forward, and hard to balance this heavy, sprawling weight.

He was breathing hard by the time he reached the car. Bending down, her arms dangling in front of him, he pulled open the back door. Then he bent lower until she was even with the seat, and he lurched forward, letting her go tumbling off his shoulders and onto the car seat.

She landed face down. He waited, expecting her to pick herself up. But she didn't move.

He pushed the rest of her onto the seat, straightened her skirt, and tucked her legs in. Slamming the door shut, he leaned against the car, gasping for air, struggling to catch his breath, his shoulders aching, his broken hand throbbing all the way up his arm.

Where shall I go?

Got to think. Got to think.

Lauren isn't at home. The words flashed into his mind again.

Lauren isn't at home. She's picking me up at my house.

So he'd take Shannon to Lauren's house. The back door was always unlocked. He'd hide her down in the cellar. Just for a short while. Just long enough for him to start thinking clearly again.

Having this plan made him feel a little better. He stepped away from the car and started to walk around it to the driver's side. He opened the car door, but dropped the keys onto the street.

He found them easily, then climbed behind the wheel.

"Are you still back there?" he called, struggling to slip the key into the ignition with his trembling hand.

No answer.

"Have you put your seatbelt on?" he asked.

Again no answer.

He glanced at her in the rearview mirror. She still lay face down, her hair splayed out at odd angles all around her head.

"I know you're breathing," he called back to her. "I'm just not thinking clearly."

But that would change as soon as he dropped her off at Lauren's. He'd leave her in the basement, in the cedar wardrobe in the rec room. Then he'd go somewhere quiet and think.

The drive to Lauren's was another blur. There didn't seem to be much traffic on the road. Or maybe he just didn't see the other cars.

It seemed like an instantaneous trip to him. A second later, he had pulled up the smooth, curving drive to the back of Lauren's house.

The house was dark except for the outside lights, front

and back. A spotlight above the middle door on the three-car garage shone in his eyes. He climbed out of the car to get away from it.

No one is home, he realized, peering into the back windows.

Breathing a sigh of relief, he opened the rear car door. Then he bent down and started to pull Shannon out of the car. It took a long time to get her back onto his shoulders. For some reason, she seemed much heavier now. By the time he reached the back door, he was breathing noisily, and bathed in sweat.

His entire body ached. He shifted her on his shoulders and reached for the doorknob. She was draped over his shoulders now, like a shawl, her arms dangling down to his right, her legs to his left.

He turned the knob. And breathed a sigh of relief as the door pushed open.

Yes. Unlocked as usual.

He stepped forward, but her arms and legs caught on the sides of the door. Backing up, he turned sideways and slipped into the dark kitchen.

It was warm inside, and smelled of baked apples.

For a long moment, he stood in the doorway, inhaling the sweet smell, waiting for his eyes to adjust to the dark, balancing Shannon on his shoulders.

I'm starting to feel better already, he thought.

Just being away from her house has helped.

Now I'll take her down to the basement and work out what to do.

He turned carefully to the wall and clicked on the kitchen light.

Then, balancing Shannon awkwardly, he turned around.

And as he turned, Lauren, Walker, the DeMarcos, his mother, and about twenty or thirty other friends jumped up from behind the kitchen units, all shouting in unison: "SURPRISE!"

Twenty-Three

"**H**appy birthday!" Lauren cried, and then her eyes bulged and her mouth dropped open in horror as she saw the girl's body around Jack's shoulders.

Jack reeled back and stared into the crowd of familiar faces. Their smiles seemed to fade in slow motion as their expressions changed to horror and confusion.

Shannon slid off his shoulders and hit the floor with a soft thud. She groaned as she hit the floor and her eyes opened. "Huh?" she cried groggily.

"I knew she wasn't dead," Jack said aloud.

The shock of seeing Lauren and everyone was helping to snap his mind back to normal.

"Jack – who is that? What's going on?" Mr DeMarco demanded. He hurried over and knelt down beside Shannon, who was groaning loudly, lying on her back behind Jack.

"It – it's hard to explain," Jack said, feeling dizzy and weak.

Everything that had happened was coming back to him all at once. He was finally thinking clearly.

"I thought I'd killed her," he said.

There were loud gasps. Everyone started to talk at once.

Walker came over and put a hand on Jack's shoulder. "I recognize her, man," he said quietly. "She's the one who did your hand."

"I really can't talk about it now," Jack said, turning to watch Mr DeMarco, who was still tending to Shannon.

"Jack – who is she?" Lauren demanded.

"I think I need to sit down," Jack said weakly.

Her features drawn with worry and confusion, Lauren took his arm and started to lead him out of the kitchen. The counter, Jack noticed as they passed, was piled high with colourfully-wrapped birthday presents.

"We didn't even have time to get the presents organized," Lauren muttered. "How did you know we were here?"

"I didn't," Jack said honestly. He decided he was going to be completely honest with her, completely honest from now on. He'd tell her everything, and pray that she'd forgive him.

She led him to the kitchen table and pulled out a chair for him. He dropped down onto it gratefully, his head spinning, the loud, excited voices echoing in his ears.

Across the room, Shannon was on her feet. Mr DeMarco

was holding her by the arm. She was tugging at her hair, pulling it behind her shoulders.

"Who is she?" Lauren demanded, standing beside Jack, staring across the room as Shannon talked to Mr DeMarco and several others.

"She's a girl from our school," Jack said quietly. "I met her at Homecoming, the night you were away. In Paris. I did a really rubbish thing. I – I took her out while you were gone."

"You what?" Lauren looked down at him in surprise.

"It's a long story," he said. "I feel really bad. I'm really sorry. But she – she's crazy, Lauren. She wouldn't leave me alone. She killed Ernie, and she broke my hand. She killed your cat, too, and . . ."

He stopped his explanation and jumped to his feet, his eyes growing wide with fear.

Across the kitchen, Shannon had stepped away from Mr DeMarco. As Jack watched, she darted over to the pile of birthday presents, her eyes wild, her expression hard and determined. Without saying a word, she tore the blue and green ribbons off a pair of ski poles propped against the counter.

She grabbed a ski pole by the handle, letting its companion drop to the floor. Her eyes moved slowly around the room until they found Jack.

"Whoa! Hold on!" Jack heard Walker yell from somewhere across the kitchen.

Jack stepped away from Lauren and called to Shannon. "What are you doing?"

She didn't answer him. She glared at him with pure hatred, and raised the pointed end of the ski pole towards him.

"You're not my baby any more!" she screamed, her voice loud and raspy, unlike any sound he had ever heard from her before.

"Shannon, wait . . ." he cried.

But she came rushing at him, holding the ski pole like a sword.

"No!" he cried, frozen to the spot, realizing she meant to kill him.

Screaming at the top of her lungs, she lunged towards him.

He dodged, and the pointed ski pole slid a few centimetres past his side and rammed the wall with a loud *crack*. The handle flew out of Shannon's hand. But she quickly picked it up and came after Jack again.

"No, Shannon – please!" He turned and ran across the kitchen. The back door was open. He heaved himself towards it, thinking only of escape.

And then he stopped short.

Shannon's enormous brother stood on the other side, his face twisted in menace.

Twenty-Four

Jack backed away from the door. "She's OK! I didn't kill her!" he screamed.

Behind him, Mr DeMarco and several others were wrestling the ski pole from Shannon's hands. She was screaming and struggling to keep it away from them.

"Your sister is OK," Jack repeated, his trembling voice revealing his fear as the big man pushed open the door and came towards him.

"Sister?" the man asked in his high-pitched voice. He stared at Jack questioningly and reached into his pocket.

He's got a gun! Jack thought, stumbling backwards.

"Look out – he's going to shoot!" Jack screamed.

But the man pulled a small leather card holder out of his pocket and flipped it open, revealing a police badge. "Lieutenant Jarmusch, juvenile division," he said, and quickly replaced the badge.

Then he bounded across the room, moving very fast for someone of his size, and grabbed Shannon by both shoulders.

She stopped screaming and struggling. She seemed to recognize him. "Uh-oh," she said quietly, rolling her eyes.

"Is everyone OK?" Jarmusch asked, holding Shannon firmly, looking around at the startled faces. "This one can be dangerous," he said.

"Uh-oh," Shannon repeated, shaking her head. "Busted again."

"You – you're not her brother?" Jack asked, his head still spinning.

"Brother?" The big police officer laughed, a high, wheezy laugh. "She doesn't have any brothers. No family at all, as far as I can tell." His expression changed. He looked accusingly at Jack. "I've been trying to talk to you, son."

"I – I thought you were her brother," Jack said, embarrassed.

"Uh-oh," Shannon said and laughed scornfully at Jack.

"This one was sent up for manslaughter," Jarmusch said, holding tightly to Shannon's shoulders. "But she only did juvenile time. You know. Like ten minutes." He sniggered, shaking his head.

"She's been seeing her parole officer regularly. Has her parole officer convinced that she's got her act together. But I had a hunch she was up to no good again. So I've been doing a little surveillance work on her in my spare time. Spare time? That's a joke."

"Uh-oh," Shannon muttered. "He made a joke."

"Just chill out," Jarmusch told Shannon. "It took me till yesterday to get a legal search warrant for her house. Just as I suspected, she's been lying to us about living with her mother. She's all alone in there. No family. Nobody. I've been trying to get enough hard evidence to show that she still needs help. I don't want her to do more time. I just want her to get the treatment she needs."

Shannon puckered her lips and, looking at Jack, made loud kissing noises.

Jack looked away.

Jarmusch did a little more explaining, told Jack he'd need a statement from him tomorrow, then led Shannon away. She didn't resist, looking back longingly at Jack before disappearing through the back door, followed by the bulky policeman.

"I think maybe we'd better postpone this birthday party," Mr DeMarco announced when they had gone. "I think we're all too confused to feel like celebrating."

Jack slumped at the kitchen table as everyone filed out, retrieving their coats from the cupboard. His mother stopped to put a hand on his shoulder. "Are you coming home now?"

"Soon," Jack said. "I want to talk to Lauren first."

When everyone had left, Lauren, sitting across the table from Jack, shook her head. "You sure know how to pick 'em," she said dryly.

He looked up at her guiltily. "Don't be angry with me, OK?"

She reached across the table and squeezed his hand. "Maybe we're just trying to do things too soon, you know." Her face grew serious. "We've been acting like an old, married couple since we were twelve. Maybe it's a mistake."

"I'm the only one who made a mistake," he said softly.

"We don't have to talk about it tonight," she said, still holding his hand. A smile slowly spread across her face. "I'm just angry that that girl spoiled my birthday present for you."

"Present? What present?" he asked.

"The ski poles, of course!"

They both laughed.

"What a birthday!" Jack exclaimed.

"Well," said Lauren thoughtfully, "I'll tell you one thing. This was one surprise party that was a *surprise* – for everyone!"

They were both still smiling as she walked him out to his car to say goodnight.